COWBOY KEEPER

Blaecleah Brothers 2

Stormy Glenn

EROTIC ROMANCE

Siren Publishing, Inc.
www.SirenPublishing.com

A SIREN PUBLISHING BOOK
IMPRINT: Erotic Romance

COWBOY KEEPER
Copyright © 2011 by Stormy Glenn

ISBN-10: 1-61034-375-1
ISBN-13: 978-1-61034-375-6

First Printing: February 2011

Cover design by Jinger Heaston
All cover art and logo copyright © 2011 by Siren Publishing, Inc.

Printed in the U.S.A.

PUBLISHER
Siren Publishing, Inc.
www.SirenPublishing.com

COWBOY KEEPER

Blaecleah Brothers 2

STORMY GLENN
Copyright © 2011

Chapter 1

"What are you doing, Billy?"

Billy swung around from where he was watching the wedding reception across the field. Terror filled him when he spotted Rourke Blaecleah standing behind him. As much as he wanted to take in the man's tall, sexy form, Billy knew his ass was in trouble, big trouble.

"I wasn't doing anything, swear," Billy said quickly as he started backing up into the woods. He had been standing just on the edge of the forest behind a large tree. "I just wanted to see. I wasn't causing any trouble."

"You're trespassing, Billy."

"I'll leave." Billy continued to back up, but he wasn't getting any further away from Rourke. The man took a step forward for every step Billy took back. "I swear I wasn't causing any trouble, Rourke. I just wanted to see the wedding."

"You weren't invited, Billy."

Billy swallowed. In his mind, Billy knew he'd never be invited to one of the Blaecleah celebrations, but in his heart, he ached to attend them all. The Blaecleah family was known far and wide as being close-knit, each member caring for the others in some way. That connection between them fascinated Billy.

"What do you have there, Billy?"

Billy instantly hid the small faded picture he held in his hand behind his back. His stomach started to roll as Rourke walked closer to him, a peculiar expression on his face that Billy couldn't quite make out.

Besides the workings of the Blaecleah family, Billy was most intrigued by Rourke. He was the third brother born of five, the middle son so to speak. Billy started having strange feelings for the man about the time he turned sixteen years old.

In the five years since, that fascination hadn't faded a bit. It had just grown stronger. Rourke dominated every single one of Billy's fantasies. He'd never met another man or woman that drew him like Rourke did. He sometimes wondered if he ever would.

Rourke suddenly stood in front of him. Billy cringed as Rourke reached for the photo he held behind his back. He squirmed to get away, to keep the picture from Rourke. He would be humiliated if Rourke discovered that he had a picture of him, even as faded and worn as it was.

"Please, it's mine," Billy whimpered when Rourke grabbed a hold of it and tugged. "It's mine!"

Billy wasn't strong enough to keep Rourke from taking anything from him. The picture was no exception. The man topped him by at least half a foot and a hundred pounds. Rourke was also thick and muscular to Billy's slim and lanky. Billy didn't have a chance.

He groaned as Rourke ripped the picture out of his hand. His humiliation started the moment Rourke looked at the picture then arched an eyebrow at him. And something in Rourke's face told him that it would never end.

Rourke Blaecleah had ammunition to use against him, and the man wasn't above using it to get what he wanted. "Why do you have a picture of me, Billy?"

Billy shrugged, refusing to meet Rourke's curious gaze. He knew what he'd see if he did, and Billy didn't think he could handle it, not right now. Billy knew what sort of reputation he had. He was considered a troublemaker.

And, in a way he was. He learned at a very early age to do whatever his older brother, Clem, told him to do or face the consequences. That meant he had gotten into a lot of fights, broken some laws, and generally made himself into someone he knew Rourke would never take a liking to. None of the Blaecleah family would.

The air in Billy's lungs got caught somewhere in mid-breath when Rourke suddenly stepped forward and pressed him up against the large tree behind him. Billy could feel the hard bark digging into his skin through his thin shirt. He knew if Rourke pushed, he would have scratches on his back.

Rourke just seemed to lean into him, not pushing too hard but enough that Billy couldn't get away. Billy turned his head to the side when Rourke leaned down close to him. He swallowed hard when he felt Rourke's warm breath blow across his cheek.

"I believe I asked you a question, Billy," Rourke said softly. "Why do you have a picture of me? And don't lie to me, Billy. I'll know if you do."

"I found it," Billy said quickly. It was the truth. He had found the small picture. Of course, he'd found it inside the glove compartment of Ma Blaecleah's car, which Clem had ordered him to search for money or anything they could sell.

Billy's knees had almost buckled when he came across the small photo of Rourke, the main character in all of his dreams. It had been taken just a couple of years earlier on the Blaecleah front porch.

Rourke had been dressed in cowboy boots and tight jeans, his chest bare as he worked on the porch railing. Someone had obviously said something funny because Rourke's head was tossed back as he laughed. The afternoon sun had been shining, lighting up Rourke's face. Even if Billy lost the picture, he had looked at it so many times the image was burned into his memories.

"You stole it," Rourke murmured.

Billy shuddered. Rourke was so close. Billy could smell the man—smell his rich, deep masculine scent, and it was driving him wild. He knew he wasn't supposed to have these feelings toward a man. They only led to trouble. Billy just couldn't seem to stop them.

"Now, I wonder why you would steal a picture of me, Billy."

Billy pressed his lips together and closed his eyes. He knew from experience that keeping quiet was his best course of action. Talking only got him into trouble. If he just kept his mouth shut, Rourke would torture him in whatever fashion he chose then tire of the game and leave him alone.

"You're not answering me, Billy."

The moment Billy felt Rourke's warm tongue rake across the sensitive skin of his throat, he started struggling, the cries in his mouth silent. He kicked out at Rourke until his legs were trapped between two thick thighs. Then he started hitting and scratching.

Billy whimpered when his wrists were caught and held behind his back. He wanted to scream at the unfairness of it all. Rourke only had to use one hand to hold both of his. The other he used to grip Billy's chin, forcing him to look up. Billy kept his eyes closed. He couldn't look.

"You like me, don't you, Billy?"

Billy shuddered when he felt Rourke's tongue scrape across his skin again.

"Little Billy Thornton has a crush on me."

Billy whimpered at the low chuckle that rumbled through Rourke's chest. His humiliation was complete. Rourke Blaecleah now knew how Billy felt. Billy knew from this day forward, Rourke would use this knowledge against him. No matter what Billy did, no matter how much he begged, Rourke now had the ability to destroy him.

"Well, isn't this an interesting turn of events?"

Billy squeezed his eyes tighter, hoping the tears he could feel growing there didn't fall down his cheeks. If he could just hold that part of himself in then he might be able to survive the next few minutes. He wouldn't let Rourke have that piece of him.

"I don't have a crush on you," Billy snapped as he opened up his eyes to glare at Rourke. He tried to put every hateful feeling, every bit of anger and rage inside of him into his eyes. It did no good. Rourke just chuckled.

"Let's just see about that, shall we?"

Billy's bravado fled in an instant as Rourke slammed their mouths together. He'd never been kissed before, but he'd imagined it plenty of times. None of those fantasies came anywhere close to how it felt to be kissed by Rourke.

Billy cried out and pushed himself against Rourke. He could feel every thick, sinewy muscle, every dip and curve of Rourke's body. And all of it felt glorious to Billy. He pulled on his hands until Rourke released them and reached around to grab on to the man's shirt, pulling himself closer.

Billy felt Rourke's hands cup his ass, lifting him up until their hard cocks pressed together. He groaned and lifted his legs, wrapping them around Rourke's waist. The hard bark pressed into his back, scraping against his skin. Billy didn't care. He was right where he'd fantasized about being for years.

Rourke pushed harder against him, their cocks rubbing together through their jeans. Even that brief contact was enough to make Billy ache and want more. Billy's head dropped back against the tree when Rourke left his lips and started kissing a line along his jaw to his throat.

Rourke's teeth clamped down on his throat. Billy stiffened and cried out, saturating the front of his jeans with his unexpected release. He felt so high that nothing could touch him. He only felt Rourke's breath on his neck, the man's hands on his skin. Nothing else mattered.

"Fuck, you're a hot little piece, aren't you, Billy?" Rourke murmured against Billy's throat.

Billy's blood went from raging hot and needy to ice cold in the second it took for Rourke's words to register in his brain. He almost choked on the cry that he tried to swallow as he pushed at Rourke's body and dropped his feet to the ground.

Rourke was only playing with him. He didn't feel the earth move. He didn't come in his pants. He didn't feel in that one single moment in time like someone might have loved him for just a moment. For Rourke, it had all been a game in humiliation.

Tears filled his eyes, and this time, he was unable to prevent them from falling down his cheeks. Rourke had taken away the one good thing Billy had in his life and made it cheap and dirty. Billy wasn't sure he'd ever forgive Rourke.

There must have been something in Billy's face because Rourke looked confused as his arms dropped away. His eyebrows drew together in a deep frown. "Billy?"

"I hate you."

"Billy!"

Billy grabbed the photograph out of Rourke's hand and tore it in two, just as Rourke had done to his heart. Rourke's mouth snapped shut as if his confusion had just turned to anger, but Billy didn't care. In that moment, he truly did hate Rourke.

Billy moved around the tree trunk and started backing away. He knew if he could just get far enough away from Rourke, he could run, and that was something Billy knew how to do very well. It was the one time he was glad he was so small. He could run very fast.

"Billy, let's talk about this," Rourke said, his hand held out in front of him.

Billy shook his head and continued to back away. There was nothing Rourke could say that would make any of this any better. He'd said everything already. Billy knew exactly what the man thought of him.

"Billy, come on, I didn't mean it."

And maybe that's what saddened Billy the most. Rourke didn't mean any of it. Rourke had rocked Billy's world, and it hadn't meant a damn thing to him. Billy always knew that would be the way it was, but a small part of him had held out hope, until now.

Billy gave Rourke one last long look, knowing that the moment he left this small cove of trees, everything would be over. There would be no going back. He'd be leaving his fantasies behind like a piece of trash on the ground.

Billy's eyes flickered to the torn photograph lying on the ground behind Rourke. The ache inside his body was almost debilitating in its intensity. Such a small thing, a cheap piece of paper really, and it had been Billy's whole world. And now it was gone.

Billy looked up at Rourke again, noticing that in his distraction with the picture, Rourke had moved closer. Billy took another step back then turned and sprinted into the thick trees. He knew despite Rourke's size and strength that the man had no chance of keeping up with him. Billy had run from bigger and meaner people before. He could easily get away from Rourke.

The last sound he heard before the trees enclosed him was Rourke shouting out his name. Billy almost stumbled as the sound echoed through the forest. He ran faster to get away from the sound of Rourke calling his name as much as to get away from Rourke.

He darted between trees, ducked under low-hanging branches, and jumped over fallen logs. He ran until his legs hurt and his heart pounded in his chest. He ran until he knew he had left Rourke behind.

Finally coming to the far edge of the forest from the Blaecleah ranch, Billy slowed to a walk. He could see the lights of his family's farm off in the distance and cringed, knowing his brother Clem was home. His folks were most likely in town.

Billy changed his direction from walking toward the house and headed to the small creek that ran down behind the barn. He needed to clean up before he went inside the house. He didn't know how much Clem had been drinking, but if his brother smelled Rourke on him, he was done for. Clem could be merciless when he wanted to be, and he usually did, but it was worse when Clem was drunk.

Clem also hated every single member of the Blaecleah family with a deep hatred that bordered on obsession. Billy had never understood it, but he had learned not to question it either. That only got him hurt. He'd learned to not even talk to the Blaecleahs.

Billy edged around the side of the barn and walked down to the creek. He squatted down and started cleaning his hands. A splash of water on his face cleared away his tears. Billy just hoped he could get rid of the rest of the evidence so easily.

He had just started unbuttoning his jeans to clean the cum out of them when he heard a branch snap behind him. Billy froze, terror making it impossible to speak past the lump in his throat.

"I saw what you did, Billy."

Billy cringed when he heard the unmistakable sound of his brother's whip unfurling. He knew what was coming. Billy swung around so fast he landed on his ass in the cold creek water. He could see the hatred burning in his brother's eyes, the spark of insanity.

Billy started scooting back into the creek on his hands and feet as Clem advanced on him, snapping the whip in his hand. He held one hand out in front of him as if the small gesture might ward Clem off.

"No, Clem, it wasn't what you think, I swear."

"I saw you kiss Rourke Blaecleah."

Billy's eyes widened as Clem raised the whip into the air. "Clem, no!"

"You fucking fag!"

Billy screamed!

Chapter 2

"Billy!" Rourke called out again as he searched the woods for the man. He had been shocked at how fast Billy could run. One second, Billy was running away from him. The next second, Billy had simply been gone from sight. Rourke had never seen anyone run so fast.

Rourke finally came to a stop, admitting that he wasn't going to find Billy in the darkening forest. He'd have to wait until the next time he spotted Billy in town. He wanted to just go over to the Thornton farm, but he knew that was impossible.

Clem, Billy's older brother, hated him. Rourke didn't exactly know why. He and Clem used to be pretty good friends. But the summer they both turned eighteen, Clem had gone away for a few weeks. When he came back, he was a changed man, filled with hatred and anger.

Rourke had tried to talk to Clem, to make him see sense. His behavior was atrocious. It had only caused a fight between them. The rift had grown until it was so huge, Rourke didn't think it would ever be closed.

And frankly, until today, Rourke hadn't cared. He really didn't want anything to do with the Thornton boys. That all changed the minute Rourke's mouth settled over Billy's and he got his first real good taste of the man.

Rourke had been with more than his fair share of men. He even had somewhat of a reputation in the bars he frequented. He'd pretty much fuck anything with a pulse and a dick. He wasn't picky.

He had yet to find the one man that would give him a good reason to stop fooling around. He had started to think maybe he never would, and then he kissed Billy. There was something in Billy's kiss that had rocked Rourke's very foundation. He didn't know what it was, but he wanted to explore it some more.

Rourke was totally shocked at his reaction to Billy. He simply planned to kiss Billy and scare the crap out of him. Clem and Billy were both known to be homophobes. He thought one touch of his lips pressed against Billy's and the man would run screaming home to Clem.

When Billy had leaned into the kiss, grabbing at his shirt and practically climbing up the front of him, Rourke had been astonished. He'd also gotten hard as a rock in seconds. Billy tasted like sweet summer rain. Rourke hadn't been able to get enough.

Rourke shook his head, more confused than he could remember being since he discovered he was gay. Billy had been a real surprise, and Rourke didn't know how he felt about it. And it wasn't like he could just go ask the guy.

He hadn't set foot on Thornton property in years. Clem and Billy were just as forbidden on the Blaecleah ranch, which was why Rourke had come to investigate when he spotted Billy watching the wedding from the trees.

Rourke's older brother, Lachlan, and his lover, Asa, were getting married in the backyard. They'd been through a lot to get where they were today. Rourke wasn't about to let anyone ruin their special day together.

Seeing Billy had sent a note of panic into Rourke. They suspected that Clem was responsible for the barn burning down, and maybe Billy, too. Where Clem went, Billy wasn't far behind. And the two of them created a lot of trouble together.

Rourke had rushed over, coming up behind Billy to stop him from causing trouble. He hadn't expected to find Billy gently caressing a picture as if it were the crown jewels of England. He certainly hadn't expected to discover that it was a picture of him.

Rourke started back toward the wedding reception, thoughts of Billy dominating his mind. He knew he couldn't say anything to his brothers. They would die laughing if they knew Rourke had kissed Billy and liked it.

Besides that, Lachlan and Asa had a particular dislike for both Clem and Billy. First, Clem and Billy had tried to beat Asa up the night Lachlan met him because he was gay, then Clem had accosted Asa and Lachlan in town, and then tried to burn the barn down with them in it. Lachlan and Asa had reason to dislike both Clem and Billy.

Rourke could see that the wedding reception was still in full swing by the time he got back. The sun was starting to set, and he thought things would have been winding down, but apparently everyone was still having a grand old time.

"Hey, where'd you head off to?"

Rourke turned to look at his brother, Quaid, taking the beer the man held out to him. He took a long sip before he replied. He needed a minute to come up with a plausible answer, one that wouldn't make his brother suspicious.

"I thought I heard some noises out by the barn." Rourke shrugged. "I went to go check."

Quaid looked in the direction of the new barn, his eyes narrowing. "Did you find anything?"

"Nothing worth reporting." Rourke quickly put the beer bottle to his lips and took another sip as his brother turned to look at him. He could see the curiosity in his brother's face and knew he wanted to ask something more. Rourke just hoped he'd drop it.

"If you hear anything else, let me know."

Rourke nodded, knowing he wouldn't say a word. If he saw Billy on the property again, Rourke didn't want anyone there when he confronted the man. The things he had to say, and the answers he wanted, were for no one but him.

"Where's the bride and groom?"

Quaid snorted. "You know Asa's going to kill you if you keep calling him the bride."

"Yeah." Rourke chuckled. "He's just so easy to mess with."

Quaid rolled his eyes. "Just don't say anything right now. Ma would skin you alive if you messed up the first wedding she got to throw. She's been planning this thing for years."

"Have you ever thought about getting married?"

"Me?" Quaid's eyebrows shot up. "Get married? Are you out of your mind?"

"Oh, come on, Ma would be thrilled to throw another wedding."

Rourke could feel Quaid's eyes roam up and down his body. There was a slight disdainful curl to the corner of Quaid's lip. "You first."

"Yeah, I don't see that happening anytime soon."

"Haven't you found someone to wear those fur-lined cuffs of yours yet?"

"Oh, I've found plenty of men to wear them," Rourke replied, knowing Quaid knew of the kinky side of Rourke's nature. "I just haven't found anyone that deserves them."

"Deserves them?" Quaid sputtered. "Are you telling me you actually make people earn the right to wear your handcuffs?"

Rourke felt his face flush as several people standing near them paused in what they were doing to stare at him. He wanted to kick his brother something fierce. "Can you keep your voice down?"

"Are you ashamed of your kink, Rourke?" Quaid snickered.

"Hell no, I just don't think it's for everyone's ears, especially Ma's."

Quaid grimaced and looked around quickly. "Yeah, you're probably right."

"I know I'm right." Rourke grinned as a picture formed in his head. "Could you imagine the look on Ma's face if I brought one of my toys home in handcuffs? Ma would have a coronary."

"Toys?" Quaid frowned. "You actually call them toys?"

"Well, I certainly don't call them boyfriends."

"Geez, no wonder you can't find anyone permanent. You're an asshole."

"Quaid Blaecleah!"

Rourke and Quaid both jumped at the sound of their ma's stern voice. Rourke turned to find his mother standing behind him and Quaid, her arms crossed over her chest as she glared at the both of them.

"Sorry, Ma, Quaid and I were just talking. He really didn't mean it." Rourke just hoped that she only heard Quaid swear. If she had heard the rest of it, well, *he* would never hear the rest of it. His ma would give him an earful.

Ma shook her finger at the both of them, her eyes narrowing. "The only reason I'm not washing your mouth out with soap is because I don't want to leave the festivities. If I hear either of you swearing again, I'll call your da."

"Yes, ma'am," both Rourke and Quaid replied. Rourke held his breath until his ma nodded and walked off. His eyes were wide as he turned to look back at his brother. "Whew, that was a close one."

"I need another beer."

Rourke chuckled as he watched his brother walk away. Ma's interruption may have been ill timed, but it took Quaid's mind off of Rourke's love life and put it firmly on escaping their ma's wrath. Rourke was thrilled.

Not wanting to press the issue, Rourke walked in the opposite direction. He was going to avoid Quaid as long as he could, or at least until he had some answers to the burning questions in his head. Unfortunately, that required Billy, and that would have to wait.

There was a wedding to celebrate.

* * * *

Rourke pulled his shirt over his head and tossed it into the laundry hamper. He was tired but relaxed from the two beers he'd had. He wasn't a big drinker, never having more than a couple of beers at any gathering. Rourke liked keeping control of his senses.

Rourke sat down on the side of the bed and kicked off his boots. He grabbed them and set them next to the side of the bed. He started to unbutton his jeans when a shadow moved past his bedroom window.

Rourke froze for a moment before realizing whatever it was couldn't see him in the dim light cast from his bathroom. He'd never turned on his bedroom light when he came inside. There didn't seem to be a point. He was just planning on getting undressed and going to bed.

He got up and padded over to the window. As far as he knew, all of the wedding guests had left and his family had pretty much gone to bed. The two grooms lived in their own house down the driveway, and they had left hours ago.

Rourke parted the curtain with his hand and looked outside. It was a clear night, the moon and stars shining brightly in the sky. Rourke could see across the entire yard with only a few shadows unseen to him. He didn't see anything moving.

Smirking at himself for being paranoid, Rourke started to let the curtain drop back into place when he spotted movement by his truck. He peered closer until a form began to take shape. Someone was out by his truck.

Swearing under his breath, Rourke walked back across the room and shoved his feet back into his boots. Grabbing a flashlight off of his dresser, Rourke hurried out of his bedroom toward the back door. He didn't want to alarm anyone that he was coming until it was too late.

Rourke moved slowly and quietly. He knew how to sneak out of the house without being heard. He'd done it enough times growing up. Rourke walked out the back door and shut it silently behind him.

He crept down the back steps then moved around to the front of the house.

At the edge of the house, Rourke paused to get his bearings. He could still make out most of the yard and even a few of the shadows. The shadow he'd seen move near his truck was still there, near the front.

Rourke darted across the yard toward his truck. He flattened himself against the side of the truck and began to slowly work his way up along the side of the cab. Looking through the passenger window, Rourke could see someone trying to put a piece of white paper under his windshield wiper. He just couldn't quite make out who it was.

Rourke ducked down and made his way around the front of his truck. Peeking around the corner, Rourke noted that it wasn't a big figure but rather small and slim. For some reason, Rourke had the immediate thought of Billy, but that couldn't be right. Billy wasn't allowed on Blaecleah property.

Rourke crouched down low and waited until the silent figure had placed the paper under the windshield. When the figure turned away and started to sneak back across the yard, Rourke went into action. He jumped up and leapt across the space between them, taking the small figure down to the ground.

The struggle was intense, the smaller figure kicking and hitting out at Rourke. By the time he pinned the small body to the ground, Rourke had several scratch marks and abrasions, and even a few bite marks.

"Billy?" Rourke was astonished when he got a good look at the pale, grubby face below him. He had expected anyone but Billy. "What in the hell are you doing here?" Rourke glanced over at the vehicle sitting beside them, frowning as he glanced back at Billy. "What did you do to my truck, Billy?"

Billy remained silent, his face filled with mutiny.

"Damn it, Billy, answer me!" Rourke snapped, giving the man a small shake, but Billy remained silent. Rourke rolled his eyes and climbed to his feet. He dragged Billy up with him. The moment Billy was on his feet, he started to struggle again, hitting and kicking out at Rourke.

Rourke grunted when Billy got in more than one good kick. He pinned Billy against the side of the truck and reached into the back for some rope. No matter how hard Billy struggled, in a matter of moments, Rourke had the man's hands and feet bound.

Billy was trussed up like a calf going to branding. Rourke grabbed the note off of his windshield and pushed it into the pocket of his jeans. He bent down and put his shoulder into Billy's stomach, lifting the man into the air as he stood up.

Billy grunted.

"You brought this on yourself, Billy."

Rourke waited a moment, hoping Billy would talk. When he didn't, Rourke shook his head and carried the man toward the house. He knew going in the front door would wake people up. The front door squeaked. Instead, Rourke carried Billy back around to the back door and into the house. He didn't make it past the dining room table before a voice stopped him.

"Who in the hell is that?"

Rourke stopped walking, breathing deeply before turning to look at his brother Seamus, who was sitting at the dining room table with a glass of milk and some cookies. "Billy Thornton."

"Billy Thornton?" Seamus shouted as he jumped to his feet.

"Ssshhh!" Rourke whispered sternly. "Do you want Ma and Da to hear you?"

"What in the hell are you doing with Billy Thornton?" Seamus hissed. Rourke could see the anger in his eyes and knew he wasn't going to get away with a simple explanation.

"I caught him out by my truck."

"So you hog-tied him and brought him inside? Are you out of your mind?"

"I want to know what he was doing out by my truck." Rourke reached up and smacked Billy on the ass. "And he's not cooperating."

"Geez, Rourke, you're going to get us all killed. What if Clem finds out?"

Rourke started to tell Seamus what he thought of his words when he noticed Billy shaking almost uncontrollably. It started at the mention of his brother Clem. Rourke was shocked and confused. He would have thought Billy would start shaking when he slapped him on the ass.

"So what if Clem finds out?" Rourke asked. "Billy was trespassing on *our* land."

"Billy was doing what?"

Shit! Rourke turned to see Quaid standing in the kitchen doorway. He almost rolled his eyes. "I caught Billy out by my truck. I brought him inside so I could talk to him and find out what he was doing there."

"And you had to hog-tie him to do that?"

Rourke did roll his eyes this time then laid Billy down on the dining room table and started untying him, first his feet then his hands. The moment he was free, Billy scrambled off the table, backing up until he hit the wall.

Billy's wide blue eyes dominated his pale, dirty face. Rourke could see his fear. He could almost taste it in the air. He looked frantically from man to man to man. His hands trembled as he held them to his chest. Billy was terrified.

Rourke knew he'd have to go slowly if he wanted to learn anything. He held his hand out in front of him, trying to soothe Billy. "Hey, come on, Billy, you know us. None of us would ever hurt you. Ma would have us up in a sling if we did."

Rourke nodded to his brothers as he slowly started toward the frightened man, gesturing for them to come in on each side of Billy as he came up the middle. They had Billy boxed in. "Why don't you just come sit down, Billy, and we can talk about this."

Billy shook his head, his eyes getting wider by the moment. They filled with more terror than Rourke thought any one person could hold inside of him. Just when Rourke thought he might be able to reach out and grab Billy, the man dropped to his knees and scrambled across the floor.

Before Rourke could turn around, Billy was under the dining room table, a chair pushed between the two of them. Rourke chuckled as much in surprise at Billy's swiftness as in the thought that Billy had gotten past him.

He squatted down next to the table and looked beneath it. Billy's deep blue eyes stared back at him, filled with apprehension. Rourke gestured with his hand. "Come on, Billy, come out of there."

Billy shook his head.

"Billy."

Billy shook his head again.

Rourke was starting to lose his patience with the man. This game was getting tedious. He lunged, trying to reach Billy before he got away, but Billy was faster, scampering across the hardwood floor until he was out of reach once again. He turned and stared back at Rourke.

"Damn it, Billy, this is getting ridiculous. Just come out from there."

Rourke gritted his teeth when Billy shook his head again until he spotted Seamus just beyond Billy's shoulder. His brother was slowly making his way toward Billy's position from behind. Rourke needed to distract Billy. He moved closer, watching Billy's entire body tense as if he was preparing to run.

"Billy, why did you leave a note on my truck?" Rourke pulled the note out of his pocket and opened it up. He was a little surprised at the words and totally shocked by their meaning.

Beware of Clem.
He means you harm.

"Is this meant for me, Billy?" Rourke asked as he held the note up.

Billy nodded.

"Why?" Billy shrugged, but he dropped his eyes, so Rourke knew there was more to his answer than he was giving. "You've never tried to warn me before, Billy. Why this time? Why not when Clem tried to burn down the barn?"

"I'm sorry."

They were the first whispered words out of Billy's mouth since he'd run away in the forest earlier in the day. Rourke thought he might finally be getting through to the man. He held out his hand.

"Come on, Billy, come out of there so we can talk. I promise no one here will hurt you."

Billy bit his lip, watching Rourke intently, as if measuring his words for their truthfulness. He started to move forward when Rourke saw Seamus reach for him.

"No!" Rourke shouted, but it was too late.

Seamus grabbed Billy's leg and jerked him out from under the table. Billy went wild, fighting like a madman. Rourke jumped up and ran around the end of the table. He dropped to his knees and tried to help his brothers pin Billy to the floor.

He was unnerved by how ferociously Billy fought considering not a single sound came out of his mouth, not even a whimper. There was something wrong with that, unnatural. Billy should be screaming bloody murder with how hard he was fighting. It sent a chill down Rourke's spine.

They finally got Billy pinned to the floor, Rourke holding his hands down. Seamus and Quaid each held down one of Billy's legs. Surprisingly, it took all three of them to hold Billy still. He was a fighter.

"Holy mother of hell," Seamus gasped. "Rourke."

Rourke glanced back at his brother, surprised by the swear words coming out of his mouth, only to find Seamus looking down at Billy. Rourke followed his gaze to Billy's back. His blood ran cold the second he spotted the swollen and bleeding abrasions that had been hidden under Billy's shirt.

Rourke's hand trembled as he reached down and gently lifted Billy's shirt. His swift inhale echoed that of his brothers as they all got a look at the damage done to Billy's back. Someone had beaten him so badly that his back looked like one big open wound.

Long slash marks went from Billy's shoulders all the way down his back and under the edge of his pants. The back of Billy's shirt was soaked with blood. Not even Billy's arms had escaped the carnage. They had deep, bleeding lacerations on them as well.

"Damn, Billy." Rourke could barely whisper the words as an overwhelming anger filled him. He had the sudden deep need to kill someone, rip them limb from limb. It warred with his need to cradle Billy's abused body to him and protect the man from everything. "Who did this to you?"

Chapter 3

Billy shuddered, pain shooting through his body when someone's finger gently touched one of the cuts on his back. Even the smallest contact hurt. Billy's entire body hurt. Clem had really done a job on him.

It wasn't the first beating he'd received at the hands of his older brother, and Billy doubted that it would be the last. Clem could be pretty vicious when he was angry, and right now, Clem was livid.

Somehow, Clem had seen him and Rourke kiss. It probably wouldn't have been so bad if Rourke had just kissed him, but Billy had kissed Rourke back, and that made him bad in Clem's eyes, which was unacceptable to his brother.

Billy had to pay for his actions, and Clem made sure he did. The whipping itself had been intense, but Clem didn't stop there. After whipping Billy until he was a bloody mess, Clem proceeded to beat Billy with his fists and feet, kicking and hitting him until he lost consciousness.

Clem was gone when Billy woke up. Billy had crawled to the edge of the creek and cleaned himself up as best he could. He was pretty sure that he had at least a couple of cracked ribs, if not some broken ones. He'd already spit out one tooth.

"Seamus, go get Ma and Da."

Billy pressed his lips together to keep from whimpering when he heard Seamus get up and run out of the room. He just wanted to go curl up in some dark hole and heal like he normally did.

He didn't want Mrs. Blaecleah to come and see what Clem had done to him. Clem always swore he'd kill him if Billy ever said anything to anyone. Billy knew he would. He had enough experience with his brother's temperament to know Clem meant the threats he made.

"Billy," Rourke asked softly, "is anything broken?"

Billy had no idea. He just shrugged then winced when pain shot through his back.

"Okay, we're going to let you go and roll you over." Rourke gently patted Billy's shoulder. "Please don't run. I don't want you to do any more damage than has already been done."

Billy held his breath as he was gently rolled onto his back. Every movement hurt, and he couldn't keep the small cry in his throat from breaking free. Billy thought he would be laid back on the floor or at the least put in a chair. He was surprised when Rourke's arms wrapped around him and he was lifted up, Rourke cradling Billy on his lap.

"I am so sorry, Billy," Rourke whispered against the top of his head. "This never should have happened to you."

Billy just didn't have anything to say to that. He didn't exactly understand why Rourke was so upset. Billy had been beaten up before, granted never this bad, but that didn't change the fact that it would probably happen again.

"Tell me who did this, Billy," Rourke said. "I'll make sure it never happens again."

Billy could only muster half a snort, but a snort none the less. He didn't believe Rourke. No matter what Rourke promised, Billy would have to go home at some point, and then Clem would go at him again.

Maybe it was just better if he left now before any more damage could be done. Billy had done what he came to do. He had warned Rourke. He needed to leave before Clem found out he was here. He might not survive the beating he'd get if that happened.

Billy tried to sit up, to push away from Rourke, but the man's arms were like steel bands around him. "Please," Billy whispered desperately, "I need to go before Clem finds out."

"Clem?" Rourke's arms tightened around Billy. "Billy, did Clem do this to you?"

Billy closed his eyes, wishing he'd kept his mouth shut. He knew he shouldn't talk. It always got him into trouble.

"Billy, answer me," Rourke demanded so harshly that Billy cringed. "Did Clem do this to you?"

"Rourke," came another voice, a stern voice, "don't you dare talk to that boy like that."

Billy opened his eyes and looked across the room to see Mrs. Blaecleah standing in the doorway, her husband right behind her. He groaned and turned his head, burying it in Rourke's chest. Things just kept getting better.

"Now, I want to know what is going on in here."

"Someone beat Billy, Ma," Rourke said.

"Well, it damn well better not have been one of you."

"No, ma'am," all three brothers answered after a moment of silence.

Billy used Rourke's momentary distraction with his ma's swearing to push away from the man. Rourke tried to grab at him, but Billy was faster, scooting across the floor until he could climb to his feet.

"Billy!"

Billy wasn't stupid. If Rourke got a hold of him again, he'd never get free.

"Billy," Mrs. Blaecleah said softly, clasping her hands calmly together in front of her, "no one in this house will hurt you. You have my word on that. You are perfectly safe here."

Billy desperately wanted to believe Mrs. Blaecleah, she seemed so sincere. He just didn't know if he should. "I got to go before Clem finds out I'm here. I just wanted to warn Rourke that Clem is coming for him."

"Your brother is coming here?"

Billy shrugged. He didn't know what Clem had planned, but his brother had shouted at him enough about what he wanted to do to Rourke that Billy had a pretty good idea. Clem wanted Rourke dead.

"Boys, I want you to go out and make sure the ranch is locked down," Mr. Blaecleah said from behind his wife. "Rourke, you run over to Lachlan's house and warn him and Asa to be on the lookout for anything suspicious."

Seamus and Quaid hurried out of the room as their da ordered. A moment later, the front door slammed shut. Rourke just stood there looking across the room at Billy. He didn't seem to be in a hurry to leave.

"Rourke, did you hear me?"

"Yes, sir."

"Then get going."

Billy watched Rourke slowly back out of the room. He could feel the man's eyes on him until he disappeared from sight. A moment later, the front door opened then slammed closed. Billy instantly turned his attention to the last two people in the room.

"Can I go now?"

"Billy, you can leave anytime you like. You're not a prisoner here, but I wish you'd stay. I'd like to get a look at your injuries and get you cleaned up a bit." Mrs. Blaecleah smiled. "I can even offer you something to eat. We have a lot of leftovers from the wedding."

"It was a real nice wedding, Mrs. Blaecleah. Lachlan and Asa looked real happy."

"Did you..." Mrs. Blaecleah glanced over her shoulder at her husband for a moment then back at Billy, "see the wedding?"

Billy felt his face pale as he realized what he said. He really needed to learn to keep his mouth shut. "I kind of watched from the woods between our farms, but I didn't do anything, I swear. I just watched."

"I never said you did, Billy."

"I'm sorry."

"You have nothing to be sorry about, Billy." Mrs. Blaecleah gestured to one of the dining room chairs. "Why don't you have a seat? I can take a look at your back while Da makes you some tea. It will make you feel better."

Billy didn't know what to do. He didn't want to offend Mrs. Blaecleah, but he was nervous about staying, too. The longer he stayed, the more chances of Clem finding out he was here. "I need to go."

"I understand that, Billy, but I would feel a whole lot better if you would let me look at your back first."

Billy knew there was no way to get out of it. Mrs. Blaecleah was going to get her way whether he liked it or not. Besides, the faster the woman looked at him, the faster he could leave. Billy walked over and straddled one of the chairs. He crossed his arms over the back and rested his head on them, waiting.

"Donnell, would you go get me my medical kit?"

Billy winced when someone turned up the light in the room. He heard a soft inhale behind him and turned to see Mrs. Blaecleah staring at his back. "It's not that bad," he hastened to assure her. "It will heal in a few days."

"Billy, how many times have you been beat up?"

Billy turned back around, his face suddenly feeling hot when he spotted both Mr. Blaecleah standing just inside the dining room doorway, staring at his back. "A few times."

"Can you get your shirt off?"

Billy nodded and reached down to grab the hem of his cotton shirt. He hissed in pain as he raised his arms over his shoulders then pulled the shirt off over his head. Billy was careful to fold the shirt and put it on his lap, not on Mrs. Blaecleah's table. He didn't want to leave a mess.

"This might hurt a bit, Billy."

Billy braced himself even though he knew not much else could hurt after getting beat by Clem. Still, he inhaled sharply and jerked when warm water was poured down his back. He gripped the back of the hard wooden seat to keep from crying out.

"I'm so sorry, Billy," Mrs. Blaecleah said. "I know this must hurt like the dickens. I'm just trying to get all of the blood cleaned off so I can see what we're dealing with here."

"I was whipped."

"Whipped?"

Billy could hear the horror lacing Mrs. Blaecleah's voice and cringed. He shouldn't have said that. He slapped his hand over his mouth to keep from saying anything else. He just dug himself a bigger hole every time he did.

Mrs. Blaecleah must have felt his panic because she didn't say anything else or ask any more questions. She just cleaned up Billy's back, put some sort of cream on it, and then wrapped a bandage all the way around Billy's chest.

A few minutes later, Mr. Blaecleah came back into the room carrying a clean shirt and a cup of hot tea. He set both on the table in front of Billy before leaning down closer to him. "You might want to put on a clean shirt, otherwise you'll upset Ma."

Billy nodded and pulled the shirt over his head as quickly as he could. He grabbed the cup of tea and took a hesitant sip, groaning when the sweet flavor of chamomile crossed over his tongue. It tasted really good.

"Thank you, Mrs. Blaecleah."

"You're more than welcome, Billy," she said as she sat down across from him.

"Billy?"

Billy turned to look at Mr. Blaecleah. "Yes, sir?"

"I know this is hard for you to talk about, but can you tell me what happened?" Mr. Blaecleah asked. He made a small gesture with his hand toward Billy's back. "Who beat you up?"

Billy swallowed hard and set his teacup back on the table. His hands were shaking, and he was afraid he might drop the cup, and wouldn't that make a great impression on Mrs. Blaecleah?

"Clem."

"Why would your brother beat you up?"

Billy started fidgeting with the white tablecloth covering the table, drawing little circles with his finger. "He got mad because I snuck over to watch the wedding."

"Billy, you know you could have come to the wedding if you had wanted to," Mrs. Blaecleah said. "All you had to do was ask."

"Naw, Clem wouldn't have liked that." Billy took a deep breath even though it made his chest and back hurt then let it out slowly. "Clem doesn't like me being over here. He gets angry every time he finds out I've been here."

"Do you come here often, Billy?"

"Not often, no, but sometimes I need to make sure you all are okay." Billy frowned as he tried to put his thoughts into words that they might understand. "Clem gets real angry sometimes, and I'm afraid of what he might do. And I just like knowing he hasn't hurt you all."

When the silence in the room became so thick that Billy could barely breathe, he glanced up to see Mr. and Mrs. Blaecleah staring at him. "I never come on to the property. I'm not trespassing. I just come to the edge of the trees."

"You're more than welcome to come visit us anytime you wish to, Billy."

"Thank you, Mrs. Blaecleah, but I don't think I will be coming back over anymore. It just makes Clem angry and…" Billy suddenly remembered what had happened in the woods with Rourke, how the man had humiliated him. He dropped his hands down under the table to his lap and clenched them, digging his nails into the palm of his hands to give him something else to think about. "I think it's just best if I just stay away."

"Billy, do you know anything about the barn burning down?"

"I'm real sorry about that, Mr. Blaecleah. I tried to stop Clem, but he just gets so mad. I was going to come warn you, but Clem locked me in the cellar so I couldn't tell. I feel real bad about what happened to Lachlan and Asa. I never wanted them hurt."

"Didn't you and Clem get into a fight with Asa?" Mrs. Blaecleah asked. "Didn't the two of you try to beat him up?"

Billy felt his face flush and glanced down at his teacup. "It weren't nothing. Clem saw Asa at the café in town. Betty was putting the moves on him, and he didn't do anything. Clem said that made Asa a fag and—"

"Billy, we don't use that word around here," Mrs. Blaecleah said sternly.

"No, ma'am. Sorry, ma'am."

"Just don't use it again." She waved her hand as if dismissing Billy's use of a word she found unacceptable. "Now, go on, you were telling us why you tried to beat up Asa."

"I wasn't trying to beat Asa up exactly. You just don't say no to Clem when he's got his teeth into something. He really has a thing against fa—" Billy flushed again. "I mean gay people. He said that Asa was gay and needed to be taught a lesson so he'd leave town and never come back."

"And what about when Lachlan and Asa went into town? Did you have anything to do with that?"

"You mean back before they got engaged?" Billy shook his head. "No, Clem got mad at me because I let Lachlan chase us off when he was hitting Asa. I was still at home recovering. Clem don't let me go out after he's lost his temper. He doesn't like people looking at me, says people might not understand."

"I'd say he's right, Billy," Mr. Blaecleah said. "What Clem is doing to you is wrong. You need to report it to Sheriff Riley."

"Why should he believe me? The old sheriff didn't." Billy snickered. "I'm a Thornton. I guess that kind of says it all."

"You've reported this to the sheriff?"

"I reported it once to Sheriff Miller after Clem broke my arm. But Clem was really angry that time. He didn't mean to break my arm. He doesn't usually get that mad."

"And tonight? Was he really angry tonight?"

Billy shrugged. He wasn't about to tell Mr. and Mrs. Blaecleah that Clem had caught him kissing their son. That might get him into deeper trouble than he was already in. Billy glanced across the room then toward the front of the house. He needed to go.

He stood to his feet, wincing when his sore muscles pulled. He grabbed his cup and carried it into the kitchen, rinsing it off before setting it in the dish drain. Taking a deep breath for courage, Billy walked back into the dining room.

"I want to thank you for everything, but it's really time for me to go. Clem is going to notice I'm gone pretty soon, and he'll be real angry if he has to come looking for me."

"Billy, you're welcome to stay here," Mrs. Blaecleah said.

Billy shook his head. "No, I couldn't do that." He chuckled a little just thinking about it. "That would send Clem right through the roof."

"Billy, what Clem is doing to you is wrong. No one has the right to beat you up. Did you ever consider that you need to get away from Clem?"

"And go where?" Billy asked. "Everyone in town hates me, hates my family. There's no one that would take me in, and it's not like I have any job skills. I never even graduated from high school. No one would hire me even if I did."

"You can stay here, Billy," Mrs. Blaecleah insisted, "work on the ranch."

That was Billy's idea of heaven, and it was something he couldn't have. Not only would he get his butt kicked from here to Sunday, but it would bring Clem's anger down on the Blaecleah family, and Billy couldn't have that.

"I appreciate the offer, Mrs. Blaecleah, but I best be getting on home."

"Our door is always open to you, Billy."

"Thank you."

Billy tried to give Mrs. Blaecleah a wide smile, but he felt like he was walking to his doom as he backed out of the room. Somehow he knew that Clem would discover he'd been here and all hell would break out. But he couldn't stay either. Rourke was here, and he was even more dangerous than Clem.

Billy peeked out the front door before opening it and walking out. He didn't want to run into any of the Blaecleah brothers. He hurried down the steps then made his way straight across the field that separated the main house from the forest.

It took Billy a little longer than usual to reach the woods. He wasn't moving as fast as he usually did. His sides hurt, his back hurt, hell, everything hurt. Billy just wanted to find a warm, dark place to curl up and sleep. But first, he needed to get something.

Billy made his way to the small cove of trees where Rourke had confronted him earlier in the day. He held his breath as he walked around one of the trees, only letting it out when he spotted the two torn pieces to Rourke's picture lying on the ground.

Billy hurried over and picked them up. He was stupid to rip the picture up, and he was paying for that stupidity. Not even tape would give him back the picture he had before, but it would be better than nothing.

"Billy."

Billy cried out and swung around, shoving the torn pieces of the pictures behind his back. He didn't think his heart started beating again until he figured out the man walking out of the shadow of the trees wasn't Clem.

"Rourke," he whispered.

"You're not going back there, Billy."

Chapter 4

The rage that had taken a hold of Rourke when he discovered what had been done to Billy wouldn't go away. He just kept seeing the whip marks marring the man's back, seeing the fear in Billy's eyes.

Rourke, much like everyone else, had always assumed that Billy did the things he did because he wanted to. It was only after seeing Billy's injuries that he began to think that maybe Billy did them because he had no choice.

And he was ashamed of himself for not seeing it sooner. Maybe he could have kept Billy from experiencing some of the hell he went through if he had just looked beyond Billy's troublemaking ways to the man beneath the behavior.

"I can't let Clem hurt you anymore, Billy."

"Oh, Rourke, he…he won't hurt me if I behave."

"Behave?" Rourke snapped, anger renewing itself inside of him in an instant. "Behave how? By beating people up? By stealing? By getting arrested? Is that how your brother wants you to behave?"

Rourke didn't miss the fact that Billy seemed to cringe and kind of fold into himself when he took a step forward. Billy was terrified of him, and Rourke couldn't even begin to think about how that made him feel. He needed to convince Billy not to return home first, and then he could deal with the ache in his chest that Billy's fear of him created.

"Look, Billy," Rourke said, lowering his voice, "I know you're scared. I know that some horrible things have happened to you, but I promise, if you come home with me, nothing bad will happen to you. I'll keep you safe."

"You?" Billy snorted, his eyebrows shooting up nearly to his hairline. He looked astonished. "You're the cause of all of this. Clem wouldn't have beaten me so bad if you hadn't kissed me."

"What?"

"Clem saw us. He saw you kiss me." Billy swallowed. "He…he saw me kiss you back."

"He tried to kill you because we kissed?"

"He…Clem didn't try to kill me." Billy brought his hands around in front of him. His fingers started fidgeting with the torn pieces of paper in his hands. "He was just angry. He doesn't want me to be a fa—" Billy snapped his mouth shut.

"You mean he doesn't want you to be gay."

Billy nodded.

"Are you gay, Billy?"

Billy shrugged. "I don't know."

Rourke almost swallowed his tongue at the soft flush that filled Billy's face. He moved a few steps closer, glancing down at the pieces of paper Billy held clutched tightly in his hands. He remembered the picture Billy had torn in two and wondered why it seemed to mean so much to the man.

"I'm gay, Billy," he said. "It's not something you need to be ashamed of."

"Clem says it's wrong."

"Clem is an idiot, Billy, and a bully. He uses his size and strength to intimidate people and hurt them. Look at what he did to you."

Rourke continued to take one step at a time toward Billy until he stood within arm's reach of the man. He was elated when Billy didn't cringe from him or run. Even still, he could see the slight trembling in Billy's hands and knew the man was terrified of him.

Rourke kept a close eye on Billy as he lowered himself to the ground and crossed his legs in front of him. He gestured for Billy to join him and was astounded when the man actually did. Billy still kept the torn picture pieces in his hands, almost as if he couldn't stand to part with them.

"Billy, listen to me, please," Rourke started once Billy had settled down, "what Clem did, what he says, it's wrong. There is nothing sinful about being gay. Just look at Lachlan and Asa. They barely have anything in common, and they are deliriously happy together. We don't choose who we fall in love with or who we're attracted to. It just is."

"Do you?"

"Do I what?"

"Do you have someone you love?"

"I hope to one day." If he could convince Billy to stay.

"Oh," Billy whispered softly then went back to looking at the picture he held in his hand, absently fitting the pieces together over and over again as if he could will them back together just by staring at them.

Rourke was a little confused by Billy's reaction, especially when he suddenly stood up and shoved the torn picture pieces into his pocket. "Billy?"

Billy's brow puckered as he frowned, looking anywhere but at Rourke. "I hope you find someone to love someday, too, Rourke. You deserve to be happy."

"What about you, Billy?" Rourke asked as he climbed to his feet. "Don't you deserve to be happy?"

Billy's smile was rueful. "I suppose everyone deserves to be happy."

"Maybe you'll meet someone to fall in love with one day." Rourke tried to be encouraging even as a weird possessiveness came over him at the thought of Billy falling in love with some stranger.

Billy's eyes flickered up to Rourke's. There a kind of anguished sadness in their blue depths that made Rourke's heart ache.

He felt an overwhelming urge to take Billy into his arms and protect him from all of the horrors in the world.

"I need to go." Rourke felt a sense of déjà vu as Billy started backing away from him. "It was nice talking with you, Rourke. Maybe we can do it again someday. Please tell your folks thank you."

"Billy, wait, where are you going?"

"Home," Billy said, as if it was perfectly apparent where he was going.

"Billy, you can't go home."

"I have to. I don't have anywhere else to go."

Rourke waved his hand back toward his ranch. "Come home with me."

Billy inhaled softly like he was trying to swallow a sob. "I can't."

"Billy." Rourke stepped closer, wrapping his hand gently around Billy's arm. "You're over the age of eighteen. You can do anything you want to."

Tears filled Billy's blue eyes as he blinked up at Rourke.

"Please, Billy? Just until you're healed." Rourke was desperate. He would have promised Billy anything to keep the man away from Clem. "Let me take care of you until you can take care of yourself."

"I don't know," Billy whispered. "Clem will be really mad."

"You just let me take care of Clem." Rourke wrapped his arm around Billy's shoulder and tugged him toward the house. He felt just a second of resistance before Billy gave in and started walking beside him, even if he was walking a bit slow.

"I really shouldn't."

"Yes, you should". Rourke barely kept himself from growling the words. Rourke was incensed at Billy's easy acceptance of Clem beating him. The man almost seemed to think he deserved it. No one deserved what Clem had done, except maybe Clem.

Billy was silent as they walked through the trees, but at least he wasn't trying to run in the other direction. That had to mean something. Rourke started thinking about how he was going to tell his parents that Billy would be staying with them.

Then his thoughts turned to where Billy would stay. Rourke rankled at the idea of Billy staying anywhere but with him. He didn't want any of his brothers to get too close to Billy, and that confused the hell out of him. He'd never felt this way about Billy, or anyone else for that matter.

This was Billy Thornton. He was a well-known troublemaker. He'd had more run-ins with the law than Rourke could count. There were people in town that crossed the road to get away from Billy. He was banned from businesses.

How could he feel protective of that type of man? The need to treat Billy with gentleness was almost overwhelming. The sudden possessiveness Rourke felt was almost as confusing. The very thought of anyone touching Billy made Rourke's teeth ache.

"Billy, I don't want Clem beating you up anymore. If he tries to hurt you, I want you come to me, and I'll make sure it stops, understand?"

Billy glanced up, a quizzical expression on his face, but he nodded. "I'm not sure what you can do. My folks could care less about what happens to me. Clem's my brother. He's all I got left."

"Not anymore. Now you have the Blaecleah family to call your own."

Rourke grabbed Billy when he stumbled, thinking the man might be worse off than he originally thought. "Billy, are you okay?"

"Rourke, you can't give me your family."

"I can, and I do." Rourke smiled at Billy's shocked expression. He swung Billy around until they were chest to chest and cupped the side of Billy's face. "My family will adore you if you give them the chance."

Rourke stroked his thumb gently over the side of Billy's bruised face, trying to find a single spot on the man that wasn't battered. He wasn't having much luck. "Your poor face."

"It's not so bad," Billy whispered.

Rourke almost growled. "Let me guess, you've had worse."

"Yeah." Rourke was surprised by the small little giggle that came out of Billy's mouth. He would have thought that Billy would be pissed, but the man just seemed accepting of what Clem did to him. Rourke just didn't get that.

"Billy, why do you let Clem do this to you?" Billy's eyebrows furrowed, and Rourke suddenly knew he'd phrased his words wrong. "No, that's not what I meant, Billy. None of this is your fault. No one has the right to hurt you, ever. I just don't understand why you haven't tried to get help before now."

"Who would help me?"

Rourke's heart cracked from the sincerity he heard in Billy's words. The man really believed what he said. Rourke wrapped his arms around Billy and pulled him close to his chest. "I'll help you, Billy."

"Why would you want to help me?"

"Because you're special, Billy." Rourke leaned back to look down into Billy's face. He was awed by the confusion on Billy's face. Rourke stroked his thumb over Billy's cheek again as he drew in a deep breath. "And I think I'm just starting to realize that."

Rourke had no idea what possessed him, considering what happened the last time he kissed Billy, but he couldn't prevent himself from leaning down and pressing his lips against Billy's. It just felt right.

He didn't know if the small shudder that rippled through Billy's body came from fear or longing. Rourke hoped for longing and thought he might have been right when Billy leaned into him and whimpered.

There was something different about kissing Billy than any other man. Rourke couldn't quite figure out what it was, and he wondered if it even mattered. He just knew he loved it. He could kiss Billy for hours. The man tasted like heaven and threw himself into each kiss like he needed the feeling of Rourke's lips pressed against his more than he needed air.

Rourke was so engrossed in kissing Billy that it took him a moment to register the fact that Billy was pushing him away. Rourke instantly dropped his hands and let Billy step away from him. He wasn't going to force Billy.

"Billy?"

"I can't…" Billy licked his lips and looked wildly around. "I can't do this."

"Billy, I would never force you to do anything you didn't want to do." As much as he regretted not being able to kiss Billy anymore, Rourke knew that forcing him to do anything would cause more harm than good. "If you don't want to kiss me, you don't have to."

"It's not that, I just…" Billy gripped his hands together, holding them against his chest. "I should go, you know?"

Rourke clenched his fists. "Billy, I thought we talked about this. You're going to stay with me until you're all better, remember?"

"Yeah, but…" Billy's face scrunched as if he were in pain. "I can't…" Billy shrugged and started looking around again. "I can't be a joke to you."

"Billy, I've never seen you as a joke."

"Haven't you?" Billy's deep blue eyes suddenly pinned on Rourke. "I've always been a joke to everyone. I'm Billy Thornton. I know what that means. I know how people see me and what they think of me. You've never been any different."

Rourke stiffened, momentarily abashed. Billy was right. He had treated the man just as everyone else in Cade Creek did, with contempt and disdain. Before the wedding and that first kiss, Rourke had never looked at Billy as anything other than a troublemaker.

He hoped to change that now.

"You're right, Billy," Rourke regretfully admitted. "I didn't take the time to look past your actions to the man you really are. You have every right to be upset with me and everyone else in Cade Creek. We certainly didn't try to get to know you better, but I'd like to change that now."

"Why?" Billy's eyebrows drew together. Confusion filled his blue eyes. "You don't even like me."

Rourke chuckled as he looked Billy's slim form up and down. Even bruised and battered, Billy had a cuteness that bordered on sexy. Rourke just didn't understand why he hadn't seen it before now. Maybe he hadn't been looking.

"I do like you, Billy."

"No, you don't."

Rourke could hear the complete certainty in Billy's voice. He truly believed what he said. Rourke knew he had a long road ahead of him to convince Billy differently. He reached over and pulled Billy back up against him, grinning when he heard Billy's voice hitch.

"I hadn't kissed you before, Billy." Rourke took a chance and gave Billy a kiss on the lips, nothing deep, just a quick brush of their lips. "I have now, Billy, and I'd like to do it again. I'd like to get to know the man you really are."

"I can't let you." Billy's hand trembled as he laid it on Rourke's chest. "You could destroy me."

Rourke frowned, not liking the way Billy phrased his words. "Billy, I would never do anything to hurt you."

Billy's laughter wasn't pretty. It didn't have the same joy-filled lilt that Rourke would expect from someone laughing. Alarm and anger rippled along Rourke's spine. He didn't like being lumped in with the others that hurt Billy. He didn't like the feeling that gave him either, especially knowing that's how Billy saw him.

"Billy."

Billy's eyes were wild, the blue in them bleeding over until the whites were nearly gone. He covered his mouth with his hand as his laughter took on a hysterical tone. He started to back away.

Rourke took a step toward Billy, only to come to a sudden stop when Billy started shaking his head. "Billy, I'm not Clem."

"No, you're worse."

Chapter 5

Billy felt a shudder of humiliation flow through him when he was unable to prevent his words from escaping his mouth. Rourke looked confused, and Billy knew the man had no idea what he was talking about. Rourke didn't understand how much power he had or how devastating his rejection was.

Billy knew deep inside his heart that Rourke would never want him, not the way Billy wanted Rourke. The fantasy he'd built in his head was just that, a fantasy. Rourke might want to play around a little, but it would never mean as much to him as it did to Billy.

And in the end, Billy would just be left with his memories and a broken heart. Maybe Rourke was right. Maybe it was time he started protecting himself. And he needed to start with Rourke.

"I'm going to go, Rourke." Billy was surprised by the confidence he could hear in his own voice. Pain squeezed his heart. He wanted to stay so much, but Rourke could hurt him far more than Clem ever had.

"Billy, stay, please."

Billy tried to swallow the lump lingering in his throat. He ached to stay, to believe in the promises simmering in Rourke's eyes. But he knew they were lies. Rourke was just like everyone else, promising things to get Billy to do what they wanted. He didn't really mean them.

Billy shook his head regretfully. Deep sorrow seemed to weigh him down, making each step he took away from Rourke harder. He felt like he was walking in quicksand. His life had become a bitter battle, and he was losing.

Billy's legs suddenly gave out beneath him as the huge, painful knot inside of him expanded. He dropped to his knees, unable to keep standing, and covered his mouth as his eyes filled with tears of frustration. He just wanted it all to end.

Rourke was beside him before he even realized that the man had moved. Billy shuddered deeply when he felt Rourke's arms wrap around him. He could no more have prevented himself from leaning into the stronger man than he could have stopped Clem from beating him.

"Billy, baby," Rourke whispered, "it'll be all right."

"It won't," Billy insisted, sniffling.

"I'll make it all right, baby, I promise."

Billy felt Rourke's mouth press against the side of his head. He bit his lip to control his sob of need. Billy would give almost anything in the world for Rourke to mean what his gentle touches promised.

"Come home with me, Billy."

"Okay," Billy whispered, no longer able to deny his need to be close to Rourke. A hot tear rolled down his cheek as he realized he would take whatever Rourke had to give to him, even if the man didn't really mean it. He was that desperate to feel wanted.

Rourke helped Billy to his feet, keeping his arm wrapped around his shoulders. Billy didn't really see where they were going. He didn't really care. The last traces of resistance vanished from Billy as Rourke led him through the trees.

"I'm tired, Rourke."

"I know, baby," Rourke replied, his voice hard. "You can rest as soon as we get home."

Home.

The effect on Billy at that word, and the way Rourke said it, was shattering. Rourke made it sound like heaven on earth, like Billy might really belong there. Billy swallowed hard and bit back his tears. He wanted it so bad. He wanted Rourke.

Billy leaned against Rourke's bigger form and tried not to think of anything. He was pretty good at that. Usually during one of Clem's beatings, Billy would hide inside his fantasies of Rourke. With Rourke by his side and the knowledge that the things he longed for would never come to be, Billy had to go somewhere else.

He blanked his mind and stared down at his feet, watching himself take each measured step. His mind started to wander, watching Rourke's dark tan cowboy boots walk next to him. Rourke's feet were so much bigger than his.

Billy cried out when a sudden hard shove against his back sent him crashing to the ground. Pain throbbed through his knees and radiated out to every nerve in his body. He looked up to ask Rourke what happened just in time to see the man fly past him.

He choked back a frightened cry when he saw another man hovering over the top of Rourke, throwing punches at him. "Clem, no!" Billy screamed as he climbed to his feet and ran toward the two struggling men.

Rourke had rolled over and started defending himself, punching Clem back, by the time Billy reached them. Billy jumped on Clem's back, trying to distract his brother or something. He wasn't really sure. He just knew he couldn't let Clem hurt Rourke.

"You can't have him!" Clem shouted as he swung his fists at Rourke again and again. "He's mine. I won't let you have him."

"Clem!" Billy screamed again. He pounded on Clem's back with his fists. "Leave Rourke alone. He didn't do anything."

Billy was suddenly pulled off of Clem's back. Hard fingers wrapped around his arms and shook Billy so hard his teeth rattled.

"You're mine!" Clem shouted.

"No, Clem!"

"Yes!" Clem shouted. His face was red with rage, his eyes wild. Billy shrank back when Clem leaned toward him. He'd never been so terrified in all of his life, not even when Clem beat him. "You belong to me, and I'll kill you before I let them take you away from me."

Billy's eyes widened as Clem's hands moved from his arms toward his throat. He knew in that moment that his brother was insane. It was disturbingly apparent in the wildness in his eyes. He also knew his brother had every intention of following through with his words. Clem was going to kill him.

Billy cried out when he was suddenly tossed aside like he weighed less than a feather. He landed hard on the ground, the air rushing from his lungs. He could hear the fight continue around him. He just couldn't look. He couldn't breathe. When someone suddenly leaned over the top of him, Billy shrank back and whimpered in fear.

"Ssh, Billy," Rourke said quickly as his hands started roaming over Billy's body. "It's just me."

"Clem?"

"He ran off into the woods."

"He's…" Billy clutched desperately at Rourke's shirt. He had to make Rourke understand the danger he was in. "He's crazy, Rourke. Clem's not right in the head."

"I know, Billy."

"He was going to kill me."

"I won't ever let that happen, Billy."

Billy could feel his body start to tremble as Rourke scooped him up and stood, starting toward the house. He leaned his head against Rourke's chest, closing his eyes when the tress passing them by so quickly made his head spin.

"I'm not sure you can stop it, Rourke."

"I can, and I will, Billy." A low growl rumbled through Rourke's chest, vibrating against Billy's cheek." Clem will never touch another hair on your head."

Billy pressed his lips together and turned his face towards Rourke's chest. He had seen the madness in Clem's eyes. He wasn't sure anyone could stop his brother. Billy wasn't so worried about himself, but if Clem went after Rourke, Billy would be devastated.

"Don't let him hurt you, Rourke, please," Billy pleaded as he looked up at the man carrying him through the woods. "You have to be safe."

"I'm fine, Billy, don't worry. I can take care of myself."

"No, you don't understand." Billy shook his head frantically. How could he make Rourke understand? "I don't think I can keep you safe anymore, not now. Clem is angrier than I've ever seen him. I don't know if I can keep him away from you this time."

A tense silence grew between them as Rourke stumbled to a stop and stared down at him. Billy's chest felt like it would burst as he held his breath. Rourke's mouth took on an unpleasant twist.

"What do you mean *keep me safe?*"

Billy didn't know what to think when Rourke suddenly lowered him to the ground, but a moment later, Rourke's arms were once again around him, pulling him close. Rourke's hands cupped Billy's face and tilted it up.

"What have you done, Billy?"

"I…uh…nothing."

"Billy."

"I can't tell you," Billy whispered, quickly lowering his eyes. Rourke's stare was too intense. Billy felt like the man could see right down into his soul and read every secret he had buried deep inside of him.

"Please, baby, I need to know what you did."

Billy groaned because he knew he couldn't deny Rourke's request, not when the man worded it like that. "I just kept Clem away from you, that's all."

"How, baby?"

Billy shrugged. "I just gave him other things to think about."

"Has Clem ever touched you?" Rourke's growl sounded so fierce that Billy couldn't keep himself from looking up. He inhaled swiftly at the pulse ticking in Rourke's clenched jaw. Billy quickly shook his head.

"No."

"Billy."

"I swear, Rourke, Clem's never touched me, not like you mean. He knocks me around from time to time but..." Billy shook his head again. "You're the only one that's ever touched me like that."

Rourke's facial features suddenly softened, a small grin coming over his lips. "No one has ever kissed you before?"

"N-no." The heat that seemed to suddenly fill Rourke's green eyes made Billy nervous. He'd never seen a look like that aimed in his direction. It made him feel achy, needy. It made him want to rub himself against Rourke and feel the man's hands on his naked body.

And that unfamiliar feeling frightened Billy.

"Ro-Rourke."

Rourke's expression stilled and grew serious. His hands tightened around Billy's face enough to hold him still but not hurt him. "I'm going to kiss you again, baby. If you don't want me to, you need to say something now."

Billy blinked as Rourke's head slowly lowered toward his. He knew Rourke was giving him time to pull away and say no. Billy didn't want to pull away. He wanted to push closer. When Rourke's lips finally settled over his, Billy sighed deeply. He still thought kissing Rourke was one of the most wonderful things he had ever experienced.

Rourke's hands gently moved over Billy just as his lips did, filling Billy with hot need. He remembered their last kisses and opened his mouth. The groan that came from Rourke told Billy he did good, that Rourke liked it.

The kiss became more intense. Rourke's lips pressed harder against Billy's. The man's tongue came out and swept across the opening of Billy's mouth before delving inside to explore and arouse.

Billy's mind went into overload when he felt Rourke's tongue brush against his, then it melted all together. Gentle hands stroked over his heated skin, moving gently down his back to cup his ass. Billy moaned and went up on his tiptoes.

His hands clenched against Rourke's rock solid shoulders when their bodies came together, and Billy felt the hardness of the man's cock pressing back against him. That hard cock was for him.

Him.

Billy Thornton.

"I want you, Billy," Rourke whispered as he pulled out of the kiss and stared down at Billy with half-lidded eyes. "I want to do wonderfully wicked things to you, but I don't want to scare you."

"No-not scared." Billy lied through his teeth. He was terrified, but not of what Rourke would do to him. *That* he wanted. Billy was terrified of how he would deal with life after Rourke no longer wanted him.

"But you are hurt, and that means I have to be careful with you." Rourke blew out a deep breath as if he had been holding it for ages. "I swore I would never do anything to hurt you, and that includes anything that happens between us, if something happens between us. It doesn't matter how much I want it."

"What about what I want?"

Rourke chuckled. "Your wants are very important here, Billy."

"Then I want something to happen between us."

Billy almost thought Rourke was nervous when the man swallowed hard. But that couldn't be right. Rourke was the most self-assured man he'd ever met in his life.

"Rourke?"

"You have no idea what your words do to me, do you?"

"I'm sorry." Billy suddenly worried that he might have offended Rourke somehow. He'd never been in this position before, never expressed his desires. He didn't know if there were boundaries, rules. He wished he'd kept his mouth shut once again.

"Don't be, baby." Rourke's thumb rubbed across Billy's lips. "I like hearing them. I like hearing anything you have to say."

Billy decided to go out on a limb and be honest with Rourke about what he liked. "I like it when you call me *baby*."

Rourke grinned, and Billy felt something flutter in his chest.

"Then I'll call you baby from now on."

Billy's face flushed. Rourke was looking at him like an ice cream cone that needed to be licked. The warmth in his face seemed to spread throughout Billy's body, heating him and making him feel anxious.

"Come on, baby, let's get you home and cleaned up," Rourke said as he turned Billy around and started escorting him through the woods again. "Maybe after you get some rest we can see what else you like."

"Oh," Billy panted softly, just imagining what they could do together, and he had a pretty good imagination. He'd been fantasizing for years. "Yes, please."

"We're still going to need to talk with Ma and Da about what happened in the woods with Clem. You know that, right?"

Billy shrugged, not wanting to let go of the vivid fantasy in his head in favor of thinking about his brother. "Can't we just forget it?"

"No, baby, we can't. Clem threatened to kill you. I can't let that go."

"But—"

"I will do whatever I have to do to protect you, baby. Your safety comes before everything else, understand?"

"I guess."

"No guess about it, baby. I have a lot of plans for us, but I need you in top health for them to happen. That means time for you to heal and a safe place for you to be where no one will hurt you again."

"With you?" Billy's life had suddenly turned into a fantasy. He might as well dream big.

"Would you like to stay with me?"

Something inside of Billy, something he didn't recognize, said that Rourke's words had more meaning than their actual phrasing.

Rourke was asking something important. Billy just didn't understand what it was.

He shrugged as he tried to think of any reason Rourke might let him stay. "I can cook. Not much, mind you, but I do know how to cook," he whispered. "And I can help around the ranch. I've been working a farm most of my life. I'm real good at mucking stalls, no matter what Clem says."

"Baby—"

"I won't make a mess, and I don't take up much room," Billy said quickly. He could feel Rourke's body tensing next to him and thought the man was going to tell him he couldn't stay with him. Billy would understand if that's what Rourke said, but he hoped to be a little closer. "I don't eat a lot either, and I can work for my keep."

"Fuck, baby, stop," Rourke groaned. "You're killing me here."

Billy pressed his lips together until they hurt. He'd said too much again, and he knew it. Now Rourke was going to be mad at him. Clem always got mad when he whined. Billy didn't think Rourke would hit him, though, not like Clem. But no one liked to hear a whiner.

Billy flinched when Rourke grabbed him by the arm and pulled him to a stop. Maybe he was wrong. He tilted his head up slightly and warily watched Rourke through the fall of his hair, wondering if he was going to need to run again.

"Baby, I didn't ask you to stay so I could make you work."

"I'm not a freeloader." He might not have a lot of it, but Billy did have some pride. If the Blaecleah family allowed him to stay, he'd damn well work for his keep.

Rourke sighed deeply. He closed his eyes and rubbed the bridge of his nose between two fingers. "Billy, you—"

"Baby."

Rourke opened his eyes to look at Billy, dropping his hand away from his face. "What?"

"You said you'd call me baby from now on."

"So I did." The beginning of a smile tipped the corners of Rourke's lips before they twisted into a wry grin. Rourke chuckled lightly. "You never cease to surprise me, baby."

"Me?" Billy squeaked. He couldn't tell from Rourke's tone of voice if that was a good thing or a bad thing, and he wasn't sure he wanted to find out.

"As much as I want to hand Clem his head for what he did to you, I'm almost grateful." Billy was a little confused by Rourke's words and even more so when Rourke wrapped an arm around his waist and started leading him toward the ranch again. "I'm not sure I would have found you otherwise."

Billy frowned as he glanced up at Rourke as they walked. "I wasn't lost."

"Yes, baby, you were."

Billy forgot all about being lost and stumbled to a stop when he spotted the lights from the Blaecleah house shining just beyond the barn. Things seemed to be going pretty good for him right about now, and he was afraid they would stop once they entered Rourke's home.

"Baby?"

Billy glanced up at Rourke again. "Can we just stay out here? Do we have to go inside?" he asked. "It's nice outside right now. We could walk down by the creek or something."

"Can you tell me why you don't want to go inside, baby?"

"They don't like me."

"Billy—"

"Baby."

"Baby." Rourke chuckled.

"You said you'd call me baby." Billy felt his face flush as he looked down at his fingers, absently picking at his nails. "I like it when you call me baby." He shrugged. "It makes me feel special," he whispered.

"You are special, baby."

Billy melted into the strong arms that suddenly wrapped around him, resting his head against Rourke's chest. He could hear the man's heart beat against his ear and was surprised at how soothing the sound was.

"You think I'm special?" Billy asked as he tilted his head back to look up into Rourke's rugged face. His heart pounded faster in his chest at the glint of something unknown he could see shining in Rourke's eyes. He didn't quite know what it was, but it made him feel hot and achy.

"I know you're special, baby," Rourke said. "Didn't I already say that?"

Billy licked his lips and swallowed. His throat felt dry. "Wo-would you kiss me again?"

Rourke's eyebrow arched, and for a moment, Billy thought he might have asked for something he shouldn't have. Then Rourke's lips swooped down and covered Billy's. Billy groaned and leaned into the kiss. He really liked kissing Rourke.

The texture of Rourke's lips pressed against his, the swipe of his tongue, even the way the man tasted all worked to drive Billy into a frenzy until he didn't want anything else in the world but to be right where he was. He didn't even mind the small ache in his back when Rourke's hands moved down to grab his butt.

"Do you see what you do to me, baby?" Rourke asked as he grabbed Billy's hand and pushed it down between them. Billy's eyes widened as his hand was pressed against the large bulge in Rourke's pants. He started panting, unable to keep the air in his lungs.

"You..." Billy licked his lips again. He glanced down between them even though he couldn't see anything through the press of their bodies. But he sure could imagine. "Can I see?"

"See?"

"I've never..." Billy shrugged. "I've never seen..."

Rourke suddenly growled then claimed Billy's lips with a hunger that shook Billy down to his toes. This wasn't the slow, thoughtful kiss he'd received from Rourke before. This kiss was fueled with hunger, and desire, and a wildness that Billy had never encountered. It was a little exciting, a little thrilling, and a whole lot scary.

Even with his lips pressed against Rourke's, Billy couldn't prevent his small cry when Rourke suddenly lifted him up and carried him toward the side of the barn. He wasn't quite sure what was going on when Rourke set him on the ground and leaned him back against the barn wall until he saw the man's hands go to the buttons on his jeans.

Billy swallowed hard as he watched Rourke unbutton his jeans then slowly separate the sides until his cock popped free. Rourke gestured with one hand. "You wanted to see…"

Billy took a hesitant step forward then quickly glanced up at Rourke's face. He watched the man carefully as he lowered himself to his knees and reached for his cock. He didn't want to do anything he wasn't allowed.

The small shudder that worked its way through Rourke's body when his hands wrapped around his erection concerned Billy, but the man didn't pull away. Billy took it as a good sign and scooted closer.

"You're much bigger than I am," Billy whispered as he fit his fingers around Rourke's cock over and over again. He glanced up in surprise when he heard a small grunt. Rourke's lips were pressed together, his brows drawn down in a deep frown. "I'm sorry, should I have not said that?"

"No, baby, it's fine," Rourke said. "Your hand feels good wrapped around me."

Billy flushed and dropped his eyes. He could imagine a lot more he'd like to do than use his hand, but that was just a fantasy, maybe. So far, Rourke seemed to be a willing participant in Billy's fantasies. He only hoped that continued.

"You're a lot longer than I am," Billy said again as he worked his hand over Rourke's cock, "but I think I'm thicker."

"Thicker?" Rourke's deep swallow was audible and enough to catch Billy's attention. He looked up.

"I think so." Billy frowned. "Is that wrong?"

"No." Even though his words said differently, Rourke sounded a little strained.

"Are you sure?"

"I'm sure, baby."

Hoping Rourke was right, Billy returned his attention to the long shaft he held in his hand. Rourke was very long, but Billy could fit his entire hand around him. He couldn't do that with his own cock. But Rourke was very silky, and Billy loved the texture moving under his fingers.

"Keep that up, baby, and I'm going to come."

"Really?" Billy masturbated, well, a lot, especially to images of Rourke. To know he could bring Rourke the same pleasure was mind-boggling to him. He tightened his grip and the rhythm of his strokes, wanting more than anything to see Rourke come and know he'd done it.

Soon, Rourke started moving his hips, thrusting himself into Billy's grasp. "Just a little tighter, baby," Rourke whispered.

Billy squeezed harder. A thrill ran through at the long groan that came from the man standing over him when he did.

"I'm getting close, baby."

Billy almost groaned himself at the deep growl he could hear in Rourke's voice. It made him feel achy. He kept one hand wrapped around Rourke's cock and moved the other one down to his own jeans, fumbling with the buttons until they came free.

Billy cried out as he wrapped his free hand around his own cock, stroking it quickly to catch up with Rourke. It wouldn't take him long. He was already incredibly aroused just from touching Rourke. This was a fantasy come true.

"Oh, damn, you're touching yourself, aren't you?"

Billy froze. All the pleasure he'd been feeling was suddenly sucked out of him at Rourke's words. He dropped his hand from around his cock and tried to cover himself, to hide what he was doing.

He'd been punished by Clem for masturbating before. He knew he wasn't supposed to do it, but being with Rourke was such a fantasy that he couldn't help himself.

"Baby?"

"I'm sorry," Billy whispered as he dropped his head forward. He squeezed his eyes closed when tears of fear threatened to fall. "I was just kind of caught up in the moment. I won't do it again, swear."

Chapter 6

"Come up here." Rourke held out his hand. Billy seemed confused but did as Rourke said, taking his hand and standing up. He kept his arm wrapped around his waist, his hand pressing over his open jeans. His eyes stayed staring down at the ground.

"Billy, look at me." Billy's head came up slowly, hesitantly. Rourke could immediately see the fear in Billy's deep blue eyes. Rourke reached out and cupped the side of his face. "It is never wrong for you to touch yourself if you want to. Granted, there are some places you just shouldn't do it, but it's never wrong. It's your body."

"Yo-you don't mind?"

"Well, I'd like to watch if you're going to touch yourself. It's very hot." Wide blue eyes just blinked up at Rourke. It was adorable and sad all at the same time. Rourke reached down and pushed Billy's hand aside then grabbed the man's cock.

A soft gasp fell from Billy's lips.

"Do you like that, baby?"

Billy nodded rapidly.

"Do you want more?" Rourke didn't think it was possible, but Billy's eyes grew even wider.

"Mo-more?" he stammered on a breath.

Rourke wrapped one arm around Billy's waist to keep them close then thrust his hips closer and grabbed his cock, bringing the two of them together. He watched Billy's face as he started stroking both of their cocks in his hand. The wonder there took Rourke's breath away.

"Does that feel good, baby?"

"Yes," Billy hissed.

"It's going to feel so much better when I'm deep in your ass."

Billy's eyes glazed over. The man stiffened for just a moment then his head fell back on his shoulders and a deep cry fell from his lips. Rourke felt his tongue stick to the roof of his mouth as Billy climaxed and filled the space between them with hot seed.

The quiet sobs of a long pent-up release that filled the air were music to Rourke's ears. Knowing that he'd brought pleasure to a man that had so little in his life, and that he was the only one to do it, gave Rourke a sense of power he'd never felt with any of his previous sexual encounters.

It also brought an obsessive need to possess and protect Billy to the forefront of Rourke's being. Billy was indeed special, just as Rourke said, and he was going to make sure that specialness was only his.

Rourke kept his eyes glued to Billy's face as his own orgasm took him over the edge. The intensity of his climax surprised him. It made his knees shake, and for a moment, he thought he might not be able to hold him and Billy up.

Billy's hands suddenly gripped the front of his shirt. His head tilted back up. Rourke had just a moment to see a deep hunger in Billy's blue eyes before Billy's lips claimed his. Rourke groaned and leaned into the kiss as his own spunk joined Billy's between their bodies.

When Billy finally pulled away, they were both breathing heavily. Rourke yanked his hand out from between their bodies and licked away the cum covering his hand. He glanced down quickly when Billy inhaled, only to find the man watching his hand like he couldn't look away.

Rourke turned his hand and held it out to Billy, groaning deeply when Billy sucked his fingers in. "Oh, damn, I can't wait to feel you do that to my cock."

Billy's eyes blinked up at him then he chuckled. "It might make less of a mess than this did."

"Oh, this is nothing, baby." Rourke grinned. "Just wait until I get you in my bed. I'm going to make you plenty dirty."

Rourke growled when Billy's eyes widened then glazed over. His breathing hitched and stuttered in his throat. Despite having come just moments before, Rourke felt a strike of desire shoot through him that shook him to his very core.

"Yo-you're taking me to your bed?" Billy whispered.

"Oh, yes, I have every intention of taking you to my bed." Rourke yanked Billy against his chest. "I plan on taking you in my bed, against the wall, in a chair, and on just about any flat surface I can find. I plan on taking you wherever and whenever I want to."

Billy shuddered. His eyes faded closed to narrow little slits.

"Does that frighten you, baby?"

"Ye-yes."

"I may push your boundaries a bit, introduce you to some stuff you've never tried before, but I won't ever hurt you, baby."

"Promise?"

Rourke stroked his hand down the side of Billy's flushed face. He loved the feeling of Billy's soft skin beneath his fingers and wondered if the rest of Billy felt just as silky. He couldn't wait to find out.

"I promise, baby."

Billy drew in a deep breath, the color slowly seeping back into his face and returning it to normal. "Okay then."

"I'm so glad you agree." Rourke chuckled, but despite his words, he knew he would never do anything Billy was truly uncomfortable with. He wanted Billy in his bed, true, but Rourke wanted him there willingly.

Rourke reached down and shoved his spent cock back into his jeans, grimacing when cold spunk met warm skin. Ignoring the wet feeling, he quickly did up his pants then pointed to Billy's own mess.

"Are you going to button up or leave yourself hanging out for everyone to see?" Even as Rourke said the words, he felt a rage of possessiveness spike through him, a previously unknown feeling. He never grew jealous over his partners in the past. So, why Billy? The mere thought of the man being seen naked or nearly naked by anyone else made Rourke want to seriously hurt someone.

Rourke waited until Billy got his clothes in order then reached over and gripped the man's chin in his hand, tilting Billy's face up to his. "No one sees you like this, baby, do you understand? No one. Your body is for my eyes alone."

"I…er…okay."

Billy looked a little wigged out. His eyes were kind of wide, and his hands fluttered, plucking at the cotton fabric of his shirt. Rourke personally thought he looked adorable, but he'd never tell Billy that. No man wanted to be considered *adorable*.

"Come on, baby." Rourke wrapped an arm around Billy's shoulders and started leading him toward the house again. "Let's get you cleaned up and settled in then we can play a little more. How's that sound?"

"That sounds good."

It sounded wonderful. Rourke was already envisioning Billy in his bed, preferably spread out with his hands tied above his head. Rourke could feel his cock start to harden just thinking about it. Billy would look stunning.

"Is this him?"

Rourke stopped, his head snapping up to see Asa and Lachlan standing several feet in front of him at the bottom of the porch steps. Asa's hands were clenched tightly, a scowl on his face. Rourke dropped his arm from around Billy's shoulders and stepped in front of him. The animosity coming from Asa was aimed at Billy, and Rourke couldn't allow that.

"Is this who?" he asked carefully.

"Don't fucking mess with me, Rourke," Asa snapped, pointing at Billy. "He tried to kill Lachlan."

"He didn't do anything."

"He burned the barn down with us in it!"

"Clem burned down the barn, not my baby."

"Baby?" Lachlan shouted, stepping forward to stand next to Asa. "You're calling Billy Thornton your *baby*? Are you out of your mind?" Lachlan waved his hand to the man cowering behind Rourke. "He's nothing but trouble."

Rourke clenched his hands. He felt a flush fill his body as anger swept through him. No one should be talking about Billy like Lachlan was doing. Billy wasn't bad, just misunderstood. Why couldn't people see that? Why hadn't he seen it before now?

"Yes, I'm calling him my baby. He's mine."

"He's Billy Thornton!" Lachlan shouted.

"I know exactly who he is, and he's still mine."

Rourke could feel Billy shaking behind him. Billy's hands were clenched in Rourke's shirt, and his face was buried in Rourke's back. Rourke reached back and gently patted Billy's hip, wanting the man to know he was safe. Rourke wouldn't let anyone hurt Billy, not even his brother.

"Billy is mine, and that's the end of it."

"If you think I'm going to allow a Thornton to stay on this ranch then you have another thing coming." Lachlan's face turned red with his hastily shouted words. "There's no telling what he and his brother might do. They've already tried to kill me once, Asa twice. I will not let them be a threat to my husband."

"This ranch belongs to all of us," Rourke shouted right back. He shook his finger at his brother. "You don't get to say who comes and who goes."

"He's not staying!" Lachlan shouted. "I'll have his ass put in jail for trespassing before I allow him to stay."

"That would be pretty hard to do, considering he has my permission to be here."

"He's not staying!" Lachlan shouted.

"He is staying!" Rourke shouted right back.

"Please, stop."

The words were whispered so softly, Rourke almost didn't hear them. If it wasn't for the fact that Billy gripped his arm as he came around the front of him, Rourke probably wouldn't have heard Billy at all.

"Please," Billy whispered again. His eyes were desperate and filled with tears as he looked up at Rourke. "Don't fight, not over me."

"Baby—"

"Please."

"Baby, I'm not sending you back there."

Billy glanced over his shoulder. Rourke did the same, looking past Billy to the men standing a few feet away. When Billy turned back to him, Rourke stared down at the man. He would leave and take Billy somewhere safe if that's what he needed to do.

"You can't fight with your family." Billy's hand trembled as he patted it against Rourke's chest. "They love you. You don't know how very rare that is, how important. Don't mess it up because of me. I'm not worth it."

"Baby." Rourke grabbed Billy's arms and gave him a little shake. "You are worth it."

"No, I'm not."

"Baby—"

"I knew what Clem was going to do, about him burning the barn down. I knew, and I did nothing to stop it. Lachlan's right. I'm trouble."

"I don't believe that."

"It's true."

While Rourke knew Billy was probably telling the truth, he also knew there had to be more to the story than that. Billy really didn't have a mean bone in his body. He cared too much for other people to hurt anyone, not on purpose.

"You may be telling the truth, baby, but I know there's more to the story than that. You wouldn't let Clem hurt me." Somehow,

Rourke just knew he spoke the truth. Billy would do everything within his power to keep Rourke safe.

"No, but—"

"Clem locked Billy in the cellar so he couldn't warn us."

Rourke looked beyond Billy, Lachlan, and Asa to see his da standing on the porch. His arms were crossed over his chest, a stern look on his face. "Da?"

"Go ahead, Billy, tell them," Da said. "The boys need to hear this."

"Oh, but—" Billy whimpered as he swung around.

"Billy," Da said simply.

Billy shuddered. Rourke placed his hands on Billy's shoulders to give him courage and gave him a light squeeze.

"Clem was talking, saying that Asa and Lachlan humiliated him, made him look bad in front of everyone in town," Billy said softly. "He was real mad. When he started getting the gas cans together, I knew he was going to do something real bad. I had to warn you. I tried to sneak out, but Clem caught me, and he…well, he…" Billy shrugged. "He locked me in the cellar."

"Did he beat you first?" Rourke asked, already knowing the answer, but wanting Asa and Lachlan to understand the pressure Billy was under, the threat from Clem.

Billy's head swung around to look at Rourke. His face looked incredibly pale in the dim moonlight. "It weren't nothing."

Rourke absently noticed with Billy's words that his speech always seemed to revert back a little when he was nervous or afraid. It was a great barometer for how Billy was feeling.

"Clem is beating Billy?" Lachlan's voice was filled with shock and a bit of horror.

"Show Lachlan and Asa your back, baby."

"Oh, I…" Billy's hands twisted together in front of him. His eyes started to go a little wild as they jumped from place to place to place, never staying on any one person for more than a moment. Rourke knew Billy was about to lose it and stepped forward, wrapping his arms around the man and pulling him against his body.

"It'll be okay, baby, I promise."

Billy's face pressed into Rourke's chest. Rourke allowed the man to cuddle closer and slowly raised the back of his shirt, letting everyone see the marks on Billy's skin. The audible gasps of horror could be heard throughout the small area they stood in. Rourke waited just a moment then lowered Billy's shirt.

He cradled Billy in his arms as he glared across at his brother. "Clem has been beating Billy for quite some time. None of us, including me, looked past Billy's actions to think of why he was doing what he did."

"But why would Clem…" Lachlan shook his head, but he couldn't seem to stop looking at Billy's back. "This just isn't right, Rourke."

"You don't think I know that?" Rourke snapped. "You didn't see him earlier, what Clem did to him. You didn't see him covered in blood and welts because Clem saw us kiss and decided to whip his brother so he wouldn't be gay."

"What?"

"Clem doesn't want his brother to be gay. He saw me kiss Billy earlier and whipped him for it. Just a little while ago he saw us kiss again and attacked us. He tried to strangle Billy, to kill him."

"What's this, son?" Da said, walking down the steps. "Clem attacked you again?"

"He tried to, but Billy stopped him, and then Clem went after Billy. He tried to kill Billy, to strangle him. I couldn't let that happen, Da. I had to bring Billy home with me."

"We need to call the sheriff, son. This can't continue."

"We will, in the morning," Rourke said quickly. He could feel Billy trembling in his arms and knew the man was close to exhaustion. "Right now, Billy needs a warm, safe place to rest." Rourke turned to glare at Lachlan and Asa. "If anyone has a problem with that, I can easily take Billy into town and rent a motel room, but Billy will be staying with me."

Asa opened his mouth, and Rourke thought the man might argue, but Lachlan elbowed him in the side, and Asa snapped his mouth closed. "Whatever you decide is fine, Rourke, but I think we can better protect Billy if he's here at the ranch where we can all keep an eye on him."

Rourke blinked, not sure he had heard his brother correctly. The man just threatened to have Billy arrested a few minutes ago and now he wanted to help protect him? That just didn't make sense.

"Lachlan—"

"I didn't understand before, Rourke." Lachlan nodded toward Billy. "Now, I do."

"He's still mine." Rourke's arms tightened around Billy. "He stays with me."

"Is that wise, son?" Da asked. Rourke could feel the intensity of Da's stare, and he heard the unspoken question in his voice. He knew what his da was asking.

"It's the way it has to be, Da."

"Very well, I suppose you should bring him inside then. Your Ma is going to want to take a look at his back again." Da turned and walked back up the steps. He stopped at the top and glanced over his shoulder. "Boys, I want a guard set up around the clock, two-man shifts. No one is to go anywhere alone until we get this all sorted out."

"Asa and I will take first shift," Lachlan said. "We just need a few minutes to run back to our house and grab a few things."

"I'll have Quaid and Seamus run second shift," Da said. "Rourke, you and Neason can have third shift. When the ranch hands get up in the morning, we can have a meeting and explain everything to them, maybe get a few of them to help us out. Until then, I want all of you to keep your eyes and ears open. And no taking chances. All of you are more important than this ranch, and your Ma would have my hide if anything happened to any of you."

"Da, could you ask Ma to make a fresh pot of coffee?" Lachlan asked. "I think we're going to need it."

"I suspect your Ma will be making more than that, son." Da chuckled as he turned back to the house. "Your Ma cooks up a storm when she's nervous."

Rourke chuckled, the tension he'd been feeling since Asa and Lachlan confronted him starting to drain away. His da was right. Ma cooked like a madwoman when she was upset or nervous. There was bound to be plenty to eat.

"Come on, baby," Rourke said as he turned Billy in his arms, "let's get you inside. Ma can take a look at your back, and then we can get you settled in."

"With you, right?" Billy whispered.

"With me, baby, nowhere else."

Rourke's answer seemed to satisfy Billy. He walked alongside of Rourke with no resistance. Rourke led Billy past Asa and Lachlan without a word then up the steps. He didn't want to give anyone a chance to question Billy again.

He could feel the slight trembling of Billy's body under his hands and knew the man was close to his breaking point. Billy needed a quiet place to decompress. Rourke hoped Billy found his bedroom acceptable.

"Ma," Rourke called out as he entered the house after his da, "can you take a quick look at Billy's back before he lies down? I want to make sure he's doing okay."

"Bring him into the dining room, son," Ma called out.

Rourke led Billy into the dining room and sat him in a chair. He moved around and sat down beside Billy, reaching over to take his hand. A moment later, Ma walked into the room with a cup of tea and set it down in front of Billy.

"How are you doing, Billy?"

"I'm okay, ma'am."

"Well, you just drink that tea while I take a look at your back. We'll see if we can make you better than just okay."

Rourke chuckled when he saw Billy simply blink at his ma. He had no idea what Billy's relationship with his own ma was like, but Rourke didn't think it was very good. Rourke's ma, however, was a force to be reckoned with.

Billy winced a little when Ma lifted the back of his shirt, but he didn't cry out or say anything. His lips pressed together, and his fingers tightened around the teacup until they were white. That was his only show of emotion.

Rourke squeezed his hand, and Billy turned and smiled at him. Rourke smiled back, amazed at Billy's ability to smile considering the gravity of their situation. It looked like a real smile, too, not a fake one to make him feel better.

"How's that tea?" Rourke asked.

"It's pretty good," Billy replied. "Your ma gave me some earlier."

"She does like her tea."

"It's, uh, chamomile."

"It's one of her favorite flavors." Rourke reached over and stroked the side of Billy's face with the back of his fingers. "She only shares it on special occasions."

"Yeah?"

"Yeah." Rourke smiled again. "I don't think I've had it since I broke my hand a couple of years back trying to rope a calf for branding."

"Oh, yeah." Billy chuckled. "I remember that."

Rourke's eyebrows shot up. "You remember when I broke my hand?"

"I thought for sure you had broken more than your hand when you took the header off your horse. You didn't move for the longest time."

"You saw me fall off my horse?"

"Yes. I was real relieved when you finally sat up."

"What else have you seen?"

Billy's face suddenly turned pasty white. "Nothing."

"Billy," Ma said softly, "you shouldn't lie to Rourke."

"I'm sorry."

"You're forgiven, Billy," Ma said as she patted his shoulder. "Just tell Rourke the truth. He only wants what's best for you."

"I saw some."

Rourke was intrigued by the small smile that crossed Billy's lips as he stared off into space. He wanted to know what it meant, but he was almost afraid to ask.

"I used to sit on the edge of the woods and watch you all working the cattle. We don't have but more than a few head on our farm, and none of them look like yours."

"We raise Black Angus, Billy."

"Are they from the line out of Aberdeenshire, Scotland, or US Black Angus?"

"You know about Aberdeenshire cattle?"

"The Aberdeen Angus?" Billy shrugged. "I read some."

Rourke was impressed. Not many people knew the difference between Angus out of the US and Angus from Scotland. "Ours are from the line out of Aberdeenshire, baby. Ma and Da brought a few head with them to start their ranch when they came over."

"That's cool. I think they are a heartier breed."

"That's possible."

"Well, think about it." Billy started waving his hand in the air as he talked. "You only lost like three head of cattle two years ago when we had that bad winter snow. Several other ranches in the area had far worse losses, and they just had regular cattle."

"I don't think I've ever thought about it that way."

"You're used to working with the Aberdeen Angus," Billy said. "Why would you?"

"While I believe there is something special about our cattle, cattle are still just cattle."

"You would think that." Billy chuckled. "That's like saying heirloom tomatoes are the same thing as cherry tomatoes because they are both tomatoes."

"Uh, they are both tomatoes, baby."

"But they are two different kinds of tomatoes. Heirloom tomatoes are grown for their tendency to produce more interesting and flavorful crops. They are a very commonly used tomato. Cherry tomatoes are small, round, sweet tomatoes eaten in salads. While these might both be tomatoes, they are at different ends of the spectrum, used for totally different purposes."

Rourke blinked.

"I prefer beefsteak tomatoes, myself," Ma said. "They are bigger and juicer. Of course, their short shelf life makes it nearly impossible to eat them all when they come in, but they are still pretty good. The boys love them on sandwiches."

Rourke turned and looked at his mother, blinking again. The two of them might have well been speaking a foreign language. He knew nothing about tomatoes beyond the fact that they were red and he liked them on his sandwiches.

He was also a bit surprised at how knowledgeable Billy was about tomatoes. The man swore he wasn't smart, but Rourke was beginning to suspect there was a hidden depth to Billy that had never been explored or allowed to run free. Maybe he needed to help Billy with that.

"You seem to know a lot about tomatoes, baby. That's pretty cool. I just know they are red and round."

Billy shrugged, his face flushing a little. "I just like tomatoes."

"What else do you like?"

Billy shrugged again. "I don't know."

Rourke didn't like that answer. "Surely there's something you like."

The furtive glance that Billy shot in his direction told Rourke exactly what the man liked. And Rourke was thrilled. He was even more excited when Ma pulled Billy's shirt back down and began to gather her medical kit together.

"I think you'll be okay in a few days, Billy." She sent Rourke a stern stare. "I don't want you doing anything strenuous. You need time to heal, lots of rest, and lots of good nutrients."

"Yes, ma'am."

Rourke rolled his eyes when Ma's hand gently patted Billy's shoulders then pointed at him. "Don't you let those pretty green eyes talk you into doing anything you don't feel is right, Billy. I know Rourke can be charming when he wants to be, but you have the right to say no."

Billy swung around, glancing between Rourke and Ma for a moment. "Rourke would never force me to do anything I didn't want to do. He's not like that."

Rourke wondered if Billy was correct. He wanted Billy in the worst way. He planned to use every tool at his disposal to get Billy, too, charming words and pretty green eyes included. Did that make him a bad person?

"I'm glad you think so, Billy," Ma said. "Just remember what I said and don't let Rourke talk you into anything you're uncomfortable with."

"Ma!"

"Don't you *Ma* me, Rourke Blaecleah," Ma said. "I'm not quite as oblivious as you'd like to think I am. I know what you have in that cupboard of yours."

Rourke's face flamed with embarrassment. He was mortified. He didn't have a single issue talking to his folks about being gay. Letting them know he was kinky was a different story altogether.

He wasn't ashamed of having a kinkier side to his nature. He just didn't share it with a lot of people. The only reason his brothers knew was because they'd seen Rourke at bars with other men. Hell, they'd seen him handcuff someone and drag them out of the bar. There wasn't much he could get by his brothers.

"Billy has been forced to do enough in his life already, Ma. I would never make him do anything he didn't want to do."

"No, I never thought you would, Rourke, but you might try and charm him into it. You tend to get a little single-minded when you see something you want. Billy needs to know that he has the right to say no to you without you getting upset."

Rourke was really uncomfortable talking to his ma about his sex life—well, the sex life he hoped to have real soon if Billy agreed. He stood up and stepped behind Billy, resting his hands easily on the man's shoulders.

"I would never do anything to hurt Billy, Ma. He's my legend."

Chapter 7

Billy frowned as he followed Rourke down the hallway to his bedroom. Rourke called him his *legend*, and that seemed to be all Ma Blaecleah needed to hear. After that, she didn't argue at all when Rourke told her they would be sharing a bedroom.

She had to know that they would most likely be sharing more than that. At least, Billy hoped they were. He knew he had a limited amount of time with Rourke, and he wanted to enjoy every second of it. He'd need something to dream about when this fantasy he was living ended.

"Rourke?"

"Yeah, baby?"

"What's a legend?"

He was confused by the soft chuckle that fell from Rourke's lips. Billy thought it was a simple question. It needed a simple answer. Right? He didn't understand why Rourke was shaking his head as he opened the door to his bedroom. It didn't feel like Rourke had any intention of answering the question.

"Rourke?" Billy asked again.

"I'll tell you what, baby. I'll answer that question for you in a week."

Billy frowned as he followed Rourke into the bedroom. He turned to look at the man, watching as he closed the door. "Why a week?"

"You need time to get better, and we need time to get to know each other." Rourke grinned as he leaned back against the closed door. "A week should do it."

"We already know each other, Rourke." Billy was so confused. He also wondered if Rourke was a little daft. "We've known each other since we were in diapers."

"We've lived next to each other since we were in diapers. That doesn't mean we know each other, not really." Billy took a step back when Rourke pushed away from the wall and walked toward him. There was a suspicious glint in the man's eyes that Billy couldn't recognize. It was a little unnerving.

"What are you doing?" Billy asked as Rourke walked closer, stopping in front of him. Rourke's mere physical presence seemed to fill the room, blocking everything else out. Rourke's hand moved slowly as he raised it to caress the side of Billy's face, almost as if he was stroking a spooked horse.

"There's a lot more that we have to learn about each other, baby, a lot more." A small, mysterious smile crossed his lips. "I think there are things about each of us that will be quite the surprise."

Billy swallowed hard. "Like what?"

"I never knew that you would be such a delight to kiss, for one."

"Me?" Rourke really liked kissing him? "You like kissing me?"

"I like kissing you, baby."

Billy suddenly felt like he couldn't breathe. His chest felt tight, and there was a lump in his throat bigger than his fist. He felt hot, like the air in the room had grown thick. "I like kissing you, too," Billy whispered.

"I know." Rourke's hand brushed down the side of Billy's face. "You are very responsive."

"Is…is that a good thing?"

"It's a very good thing, baby," Rourke said.

Billy almost swooned at the deep, rich timbre in Rourke's voice. It traveled right up his spine.

"I like knowing how you feel, that you enjoy what we do together."

Okay, swooning was a very real possibility. Billy could feel his knees start to tremble. He grabbed on to Rourke's shirt and locked his knees in place. If he didn't, Billy was positive he'd collapse on the floor.

"I...I do en-enjoy wh-what we do together," Billy stammered. He could feel his face flush with each word he spoke. He'd never talked to anyone the way he was talking to Rourke. It was a little exhilarating and a whole lot scary.

"Would you like to find out what else we can do together?"

Billy nodded rapidly, biting his lower lip as wicked thoughts began to fill his head. He could think of so many things he would like to try with Rourke, most of them requiring a flat surface. He'd been fantasizing about the man for years. He could imagine a lot.

"Let's get you settled then, shall we?"

Billy nodded again, although he was unsure of exactly what Rourke wanted until the man grabbed the edge of his shirt and lifted it up. Billy raised his arms in the air and let Rourke draw the shirt up over his head. He didn't even care when Rourke tossed it on the floor.

The man's hand next went to the buttons of Billy's jeans. Billy quickly sucked in a deep breath when Rourke's fingers brushed against the skin of his abdomen. His body suddenly felt hot and flushed.

"I've got you, baby."

The softly spoken words whispered over Billy's skin like a caress. He dropped his head back on his shoulders and tried not to moan like a girl. He wanted to impress Rourke, not freak the man out. But just the mere touch of the man's fingers over his skin felt like heaven.

Billy felt Rourke's arms wrap around him then the world tilted. Billy lifted his head to find Rourke carrying him toward the bed. He didn't say anything when Rourke set him on the side of the bed then knelt down in front of him, reaching for his shoes. He didn't know what to say.

The Blaecleah brothers were known far and wide as being rough-and-tumble men. They didn't take crap from anyone. They wouldn't necessarily start a fight, but they would finish one. Not many people wanted to take them on.

Gentle was not something usually associated with the five men. Billy certainly never thought of Rourke as gentle, but that's how the man was acting. He treated Billy like he was made of spun glass. Each touch was gentle, careful, as if he wanted to take the utmost care when stripping Billy's clothes from him.

A small, lonely part of Billy appreciated each tender touch, soaked it up and stored the memory away to be taken out later and examined. Another part, also the lonely part, was afraid of how much he knew he'd come to depend on those small touches. Billy knew he'd crave those touches like he craved the sight of Rourke.

Rourke tossed Billy's shoes over his shoulder then peeled his socks off. Billy groaned and leaned back on his hands when Rourke gave each foot a gentle massage. He didn't realize until then that his feet even hurt. And Rourke's touch was magical, drawing away every last ache and pain.

"Lay back, baby."

Billy did as Rourke directed and carefully lay back on the mattress. His back ached a little when it pressed down on the bed but not enough for Billy to complain. He'd had far worse, and he wasn't about to do or say anything that would stop Rourke.

"Lift your hips if you can."

Billy lifted his hips, his face flushing furiously when Rourke tugged his jeans down his legs. Billy quickly reached down and covered his groin with one hand.

"Sshhh, baby," Rourke said as he tugged on Billy's wrist, "you don't have to hide from me."

"I just…" Billy felt flustered as he let Rourke pull his hand away. "No one's ever…it's, well…no one's ever seen me like this and..."

"And, I can't even begin to explain to you how much that means to me." Rourke grinned broadly.

Billy trembled and inhaled a sharp breath when he felt Rourke's hands stroke his naked skin, slowly moving up his legs toward his groin. Not only had no one ever seen him in his present state of undress, no one had ever touched him like Rourke was doing.

"To know that I will be the only one to ever see you like this or touch you…" Rourke growled, the timbre in his voice getting thicker. "You really don't understand how arousing that is, baby."

Billy almost jumped right out of his skin when Rourke leaned down and rubbed his face against the sensitive skin of his abdomen. Rourke seemed to be breathing in deeply as he rubbed his face over Billy again and again.

"You're all mine now, baby, all mine." Rourke suddenly pushed away and stood to his feet, stepping back a couple of paces. "Watch me, baby, watch what you do to me."

Like that was a problem, Billy thought to himself. He could no more look away from Rourke than he could stop breathing. The fact that Rourke had started stripping off his clothes only made it more impossible for Billy to look away. Each bit of naked skin revealed added to every fantasy Billy had ever imagined about the man, only this was real.

Billy was already semi-hard. He always got aroused when he was around Rourke. Watching the man strip naked put a whole new spin on the lust coursing through his body. Rourke was a work of art. Seeing him naked for the first time, Billy quickly realized that none of his fantasies ever compared to the man in reality.

Rourke's broad shoulders belied the trimness of his waist. The man was definitely fit. He worked hard for a living, and it showed in every bulging muscle and every bit of taut, rippling skin. He was breathtaking. He was certainly taking the breath from Billy.

His skin was lightly tanned but unmarred by tan lines, giving Billy yet another fantasy to dream about, where the man sunbathed nude.

Thick pectoral muscles graced his chest, leading down to a trim waist and ripped abdominal muscles.

Billy's eyes started to move below Rourke's waistline when the man suddenly grabbed his cock. Billy groaned and arched into the air, the soft touch exquisite. "Rourke!"

"Ssshh, settle, baby," Rourke said as he gently pushed on Billy's abdomen. "You're still injured. We can't do anything that will get us in trouble or cause you more pain. I just want you to lie there and let me do all the work. I'll make sure you feel good."

Billy had no reason not to believe the man. Just the simple touch of Rourke's hand on him was more than he ever thought he'd have. The rest was all just a bonus.

"I want you to scoot up to the top of the bed and grab the headboard." Rourke chuckled lightly. "And no letting go, baby, no matter what."

There was something in Rourke's voice, a kind of fierce tone that told Billy holding on to the headboard was really important to the man. He was more than willing to try anything Rourke suggested.

Moving carefully, Billy scooted to the top of the bed and lay back down. He reached over his head and wrapped his fingers around the white wrought iron headboard then looked back down at Rourke.

"Like this?"

Rourke bit his lips and nodded. His green eyes started to darken right before Billy, turning a deep emerald green. Rourke's face flushed, his jaw clenching as if he was holding on to his control by a thread. It thrilled Billy, excited him, but it also scared him. He didn't know what to expect.

"One of these days I'm going to handcuff you to my headboard, baby, and fuck you until you can't walk."

Billy blinked, his eyebrows shooting up in shock. "You want to handcuff me?"

"I do."

"Why?"

Billy's breath caught in his throat when Rourke leaned over, his hands landing on Billy's chest just over his nipples. He started to draw them slowly down Billy's body, his eyes following the path his hands made.

"Because you would look very sexy handcuffed to my headboard, displayed for my pleasure."

Billy licked his suddenly dry lips. "Okay."

Rourke's eyes flickered up to his. "Okay?"

Billy nodded. "Okay, you can handcuff me."

"Bil-baby, you don't know what you're saying."

"I do, too." Billy frowned. He wasn't that stupid. "You get turned on by the idea of having me handcuffed to your headboard."

"Baby, you really don't know what you're saying."

Billy rolled his eyes when Rourke gripped him tighter and repeated his words. He did know what he was saying. Granted, he had never been handcuffed before unless he was under arrest, but if it aroused Rourke as much as he thought it did, he was all for it.

"Rourke, stop treating me like spun glass," Billy said. "If you plan on handcuffing me later then there is no reason you can't do it now. It's obvious that it's something that you want."

"Baby, you're injured."

"And?"

Rourke bit his lower lip again, his eyes moving up and down Billy's body. He drew in a deep breath, letting it out slowly as his eyes met Billy's again. "I'll be honest here, baby. I do want to handcuff you. That's something that arouses me a lot. But I'm not sure I can control myself if we do that. I want it, but not at your expense."

"You'll stop if I ask you to."

One eyebrow on Rourke's forehead arched up. "You think so, huh?"

"I know so." Billy had no idea how he knew that, but he did. Rourke would never do anything to purposely hurt him. Billy knew it deep down in his soul. "I trust you."

Rourke's eyes fluttered closed. "You really have no idea what you're saying, baby."

"Do you think I'm stupid?" It was the only explanation. Billy told Rourke he was willing to be handcuffed, and it was obviously something the man wanted a lot. Billy didn't understand what the problem was.

"What?" Rourke's eyes opened, and he looked back down at Billy. "Of course I don't think you're stupid. What would make you ask something like that?"

"It's obvious that handcuffing me turns you on. I've said I'm okay with it." Billy sat up, waving his hand a little in the air for effect. "Why are you trying so hard to talk me out of it? Don't you think I know my own mind?"

"I don't think you realize what you're getting yourself into."

"So, tell me then."

Billy almost wished he hadn't said anything when Rourke's shoulders slumped. He was always talking too much. He should have stopped while he was ahead. Rourke seemed more than willing to mess around until Billy opened his mouth and demanded more. He *was* stupid.

Billy dropped his eyes, Rourke's look too intense. "I'm sorry. I didn't mean to make you upset."

"Baby, I'm not upset. I just…" Rourke pushed a hand through his light brown hair. "I can be very intense sometimes, especially when it comes to the things I like sexually. You've never been with anyone, and I don't want to frighten you your first time out. Does that make sense to you?"

"Yes." Well, sort of. Billy wasn't exactly sure what Rourke meant by intense. "I still don't understand what it has to do with this situation. If you plan to use handcuffs on me later then why won't you use them now?"

"Because you're injured, baby."

Billy sighed deeply and lay back on the mattress again. "Okay, maybe I don't understand. I feel like you're talking in circles."

Billy inhaled sharply when Rourke suddenly moved up and hovered over him. His facial features were taut as if he were under a lot of strain. Rourke grabbed one of Billy's hands and moved it down to his cock, pressing Billy's fingers around his thick erection.

"I'm not normally a gentle man, baby. I'm trying to be considerate because you're injured." Rourke shook his head. "But if you weren't injured, I'd already be balls deep inside your ass. And I'd fuck you, baby, until you couldn't walk straight. I'd handcuff you to my bed and not let you go until I was done with you, and that would take a very long time."

Billy's mouth dropped open. He'd never heard words spoken like Rourke's that aroused him so quickly or made his body tremble so much. He wasn't sure he'd ever heard words spoken quite like Rourke's, period.

"And...and handcuffing me is bad because?"

"It's not bad, baby, but it would send me over the edge. It's all I can do right now to treat you gently. If I saw you handcuffed and knew I could do anything I wanted to you, I don't think I would be able to be gentle."

It wasn't getting any easier for Billy to breathe. With each word that Rourke spoke, he was taking away another breath of air.

"Just let me do this my way, baby. I'll introduce you to my handcuffs in a few days."

"Promise?"

"Oh, hell yeah."

Billy swallowed then nodded. "Okay."

Rourke grinned. "Okay, hands over your head again. Grab the headboard."

Billy reached up and grabbed the headboard again. He couldn't take his eyes off of Rourke as he watched the man lean down and stroke his tongue across his naked skin. Rourke didn't seem to be in a great hurry as he slowly licked and nipped his way across Billy's chest.

Each nipple was lavished, licked, sucked, and then nibbled on until Billy was squirming under Rourke, pressing himself up into the man. No one had ever touched him like Rourke was doing. Billy had no idea his nipples could be so sensitive.

Billy's mind seemed to fragment when Rourke moved further down his chest to his abdomen. They were simple abdominal muscles, a belly button. They shouldn't need to feel Rourke's tongue move across them quite like they did. Billy almost cried out when Rourke's mouth left his abdomen until he felt hot lips wrap around the head of his cock.

"Rourke!" he cried out.

His fingers tightened around the wrought iron bars so tightly that they hurt. He bent his knees and planted his feet firmly in the mattress before driving his cock up into Rourke's mouth. Nothing on earth had ever felt this good.

Billy's bubble of euphoria suddenly burst when he felt something hard and wet press against his ass. He stiffened, frightened and unused to anything touching him there. His cock was still in Rourke's mouth, but Billy could feel it start to wilt at the strange sensation.

"Rourke." Billy swallowed, suddenly scared.

Rourke's head popped up and green eyes met Billy's. "It's okay, baby, it's just my fingers. I won't do it if you don't want me to."

Billy drew in a deep breath and tried to calm his racing heart. "I've just never…"

Rourke grinned. He seemed incredibly proud of that fact. "I know, but I promise you'll enjoy it."

"Okay," Billy said slowly. He still winced when Rourke began pushing his finger in deeper. It wasn't exactly painful, more weird than anything. It took a few minutes, but Billy slowly grew used to the finger in his ass. He was just starting to let his muscles loosen, letting go of the tension in them, when he felt another finger push into his ass. "Rourke!"

"Do you want me to stop, baby?"

"Ho-how many do you plan to put in there?" Billy could feel his face flush with heat as he spoke. It got even worse when Rourke chuckled.

"Three at least, baby, but more than likely four when we do finally get to really fooling around. Like you said before when we were out by the barn, I'm not exactly a small man."

"F-f-four?" Billy squeaked. He couldn't imagine having four fingers in his ass. Sure, he'd imagined being fucked by Rourke. He just never really thought about the exact dynamics of the actual act itself.

"Let me show you something, baby."

Billy had no idea what Rourke was talking about until he felt the fingers in his ass start to move around. Again, he found the sensation not totally uncomfortable, just weird. Rourke's fingers moved in and out of him, going deeper each time.

Billy kept waiting for something magical to happen, something that would make this seem not quite so odd. Then Rourke's fingers suddenly curved and brushed against something deep inside of Billy. He stiffened, a loud wail falling from his lips as he arched into the air.

"There we go," Rourke whispered.

Billy panted heavily as he lowered himself back down to the mattress. He'd never, ever, felt anything like it. Billy thought the sensation was like a combination of the one he felt when he kissed Rourke and kissing a light socket.

"What was that?"

"That, baby, is called your sweet spot."

"I can see that."

"It gets better."

"Better?"

Rourke's mouth dropped back down over Billy's cock. At the same time, his fingers began moving again, pushing in and out of Billy's ass. Billy held his breath, overcome by the feeling of Rourke sucking on his cock and the anticipation of having his sweet spot stroked again.

When it came, Billy cried out and instantly filled Rourke's mouth with his release. White lights swam in front of his eyes as his brain seemed to short-circuit. He couldn't think, only feel. And he felt everything from the way Rourke sucked on his cock to the fingers that continued to stroke him through his orgasm.

Billy almost whimpered in protest when Rourke suddenly pulled away from him until he saw the man kneel between his thighs and lean over the top of him. Rourke had his cock in his hand and was stroking himself furiously.

Billy was entranced. He'd never seen anything so beautiful in all his life. Rourke's face was taut, his jaw clenched, and his lips pressed tightly together. And even though he stroked his cock rapidly, his eyes never once left Billy's body. Billy let go of the headboard and started to reach for Rourke until the man's sharp words stopped him.

"Hands!"

Billy instantly reached back up and wrapped his fingers around the headboard. He licked his lips. He could feel himself start to harden again even though he'd just experienced the most intense orgasm of his life. How could he not when the object of his every fantasy was jerking off over the top of him?

"You're really looking forward to those handcuffs, aren't you? You want to see me all bound up for you."

Billy often wished he'd kept his mouth shut after speaking. It had gotten him into trouble way too many times. But when Rourke's green eyes snapped up to his then suddenly glazed over as his head fell back on his shoulders, Billy was glad he had.

The loud roar that filled the room as ropes of white shot out over Billy's chest was worth everything. Billy kept his hands firmly wrapped around the headboard as Rourke dropped down to rest his head on Billy's chest. He desperately wanted to hug the man, to touch him in some way. He just didn't know if he could.

"Rourke?" he whispered.

Rourke slowly lifted his head, a small, sensuous smile playing across his lips. "We're definitely using the handcuffs next time."

Chapter 8

Rourke chuckled as he watched Billy and Ma working in the garden. They seemed to be arguing over something, but he didn't rightly know what it was. Billy was waving his hands around wildly as he pointed up and down the garden rows they had just gotten done hoeing. Ma was gesturing back.

Billy had only been at the ranch for a couple of days, but each one seemed to bring out something new in his personality. Rourke had been mildly surprised by Billy's humor, often finding himself laughing at something Billy said.

What was even more surprising was how smart Billy actually was when he opened up. Rourke had been shocked into silence more than once in the last two days when Billy said something or commented on something. He might not have graduated from high school, but he wasn't stupid by any means.

"You better go save him before Ma feeds him to the chickens."

Rourke glanced over his shoulder to see Lachlan standing behind him, a small smile on his face. Rourke chuckled and turned back to watch Billy and Ma argue. "I don't know. Ma might have actually met her match this time. Billy's pretty stubborn when he wants to be."

"Billy?" Lachlan snorted. "We are talking about the same man here, right? Billy Thornton?"

"Yes, we're talking about the same Billy." Rourke rolled his eyes and turned to glare at his brother when the man snorted. "Have you ever taken the time to actually talk with Billy?"

"Rourke."

"I understand that he has a bad reputation, but it's not who he really is. Billy is kind and sweet. He wouldn't hurt a hair on anyone's head if Clem didn't force him to." Rourke waved his hand wildly in the air. "You try living what Billy's been through and see if you come out of it as well as he has. Despite everything Clem has ever done to him, and even knowing that it could mean another beating or his life, Billy still tries to keep us safe from Clem. Let me see you try something like that."

"Rourke, I'm not saying—"

"You're not saying anything." Rourke clenched his fists together to keep from planting them in his brother's face. He was getting damn tired of people picking on Billy. "I don't want to hear you say another word about him."

"Rourke—"

"Not a word, Lachlan!"

"He's standing right behind you," Lachlan said quickly.

Rourke swallowed and slowly turned around to find Billy and Ma standing right behind him. Ma had her arms crossed over her chest and was tapping her foot. She didn't look happy. Billy, on the other hand, looked ecstatic, a large smile gracing his lips.

"Hey."

"Hey," Billy said back, his face flushing, but the smile never left his lips.

"How's the gardening going?"

Ma snorted and rolled her eyes. "Billy seems to think that growing tomatoes next to the fence is better than the pots I have by the back porch."

Rourke bit his lip. He wasn't about to enter a conversation concerning his Ma's garden. He wasn't that stupid. He was shocked when Billy turned to look at Ma, gesturing with his hands again.

"But the fence is better. I know you said you liked the beefsteak tomatoes, and those are great tomatoes, but have you ever eaten a tomato fresh off the vine? There's nothing like it."

"I still don't see the difference in growing the tomatoes by the fence or in the pots."

"If you grow vine tomatoes by the fence, they can use the fence to grow up towards the sun. Tomatoes love the sun. And the fence will help protect them from the elements. Up on the porch, even in the pots, they are at the mercy of the weather."

Ma opened her mouth as if to reply then snapped it shut. She glanced back at the garden for several minutes then looked back at Billy. "Okay, I see what you're saying, but I still like having my tomatoes in pots on the back porch."

"So, why don't we plant a little of both then. You can grow some by the fence and grow some in the pots." Billy shrugged. "It's not like you can have too many tomatoes."

"You know, Billy, that's not a bad idea. That way, I can see which grows best." Ma smiled and turned back to her garden, walking off in that direction. "Come on, son, we have some planting to do."

Billy smiled and started to follow after Ma. He suddenly stopped and turned, running back toward Rourke. Billy leaned up on his tiptoes and placed a small kiss on Rourke's lips. "Thanks for believing in me," Billy whispered as he dropped back down to his feet.

Rourke smiled and tapped Billy on the nose. "I'll always believe in you, baby."

Billy's grin was brighter than the sun. He laughed and turned, running toward Ma's garden. Rourke felt lighter as he watched Billy run over to join his ma. He couldn't help laughing when Billy and Ma started arguing the moment Billy hopped over the fence.

He doubted the two of them would ever stop arguing, but it seemed to be all in good fun, never harmful. And maybe Billy needed that. He needed to see that he was accepted no matter what. Rourke would have to work on that.

"He certainly seems to have you caught in his net, baby brother."

"He's my legend," Rourke said without looking away from Billy.

"Well, shit." Lachlan chuckled. "I guess that means I'm going to have to be nice to the guy."

"It does."

"Does he know?"

"No, not yet," Rourke said. He reluctantly tore his eyes away from Billy and went back to stacking hay. "I'll tell him when the time is right."

"Don't wait too long, Rourke. You don't want to take the chance of losing him. Believe me. I know what I'm talking about."

Rourke quickly glanced over at his brother as Lachlan grabbed the hay bale next to him. The seriousness of the expression on Lachlan's face told him that his brother knew exactly what he was talking about.

"I won't. I'll tell him as soon as I can. I don't want to do anything that would cause me to lose Billy."

Lachlan nodded then chuckled. "That's going to take some time getting used to, my brother and Billy Thornton. Who would have thought of it?"

"Yeah, surprised the shit out of me, too."

* * * *

Rourke knew something was different the moment he woke up. After spending the last few days waking up with Billy wrapped in his arms, waking up alone was kind of alarming. He opened his eyes and glanced around the room, instantly spotting Billy standing by the dresser.

"What are you doing, baby?"

Billy swung around, his face paling as he hid his hands behind his back. "Nothing."

Rourke arched an eyebrow. "What are you hiding behind your back then?"

Billy's face paled even more. Rourke also noticed that the man refused to meet his eyes. He stared anywhere except at Rourke.

"Nothing."

Rourke sighed and scooted up against the headboard. He folded his hands together in his lap. Rourke had spent nearly every waking moment with Billy over the last few days, and even his sleeping ones. He thought he and Billy had been making progress.

They'd talked, and cuddled, and even fooled around a bit as Billy healed. While his body was healing pretty well, Billy was still a mass of bruises—very colorful bruises at this point. Rourke knew he would need several more days, if not a couple of weeks, to be in fit condition.

Luckily for Rourke, his brothers had all pitched in to take over the bulk of his work on the ranch, enabling him to spend as much time as possible with Billy. Rourke knew that wouldn't go on forever, but he was grateful for the time they did give him.

"Come here, baby." Rourke crooked his finger at Billy then watched as the man reluctantly shuffled forward. Billy stopped at the edge of the bed. Rourke held out his hand and waited. Billy slowly brought his hands around in front of him.

Rourke was shocked to see his fur-lined handcuffs locked around one of Billy's wrists. He hooked his finger through the empty cuff and jerked on it, pulling Billy forward until he had to either climb up on the bed or fall on it.

"What have you done, baby?"

Billy shrugged and crawled into the space between Rourke's legs. He settled back against Rourke's chest and started fidgeting with the cuffs. "I just wanted to see what they felt like. I didn't do anything wrong."

"I told you we would use the handcuffs in a few days."

"You also told me that we would use them the next time we fooled around, and we didn't."

Rourke loved the defiance he could hear in Billy's voice. Over the last few days, Billy had started to argue with him more and more. He never raised his voice or became violent, but he was starting to state his likes and dislikes on a more consistent basis. Rourke saw that as a good start to Billy's recovery.

Rourke picked Billy up in his arms. He swung him around until Billy straddled his legs and they were facing each other. He grinned down into Billy's shocked face as he grabbed the empty handcuff in one hand and Billy's bare wrist in the other, pulling both behind Billy's back.

Even if he hadn't felt Billy's cock harden against his abdomen, Rourke would have known Billy was aroused. Billy had tell signs. He inhaled softly. His blue eyes darkened. The pulse in his neck beat rapidly. These were all signs Rourke had come to recognize.

"You've really been thinking about this, haven't you?"

Billy shrugged, his eyes dropping down. "You said you would, and you haven't and…"

"I know, but I wanted to give you just a few more days to heal up while we played around and got you used to me."

Billy's eyes snapped up. "I am used to you."

"You think so, huh?" Rourke smirked and reached over to the end table, pulling the drawer open. He searched around with his hand until it closed over a small bottle of lube and a condom, pulling both out before closing the drawer.

He dropped the bottle and condom on the bed then pulled Billy's hands around in front of him. Rourke heard Billy's soft inhale as he attached the loose handcuff to Billy's bare wrist then draped the bound hands over his neck. Billy couldn't have pulled away even if he had wanted to.

"Are you sure you're ready for me, baby?"

Billy swallowed hard and nodded.

Rourke chuckled as he lifted Billy up just a little and pushed the blanket away, kicking it to the end of the bed with his feet. He settled Billy back down in his lap, their naked bodies pressing together. Rourke almost groaned when his hard cock pushed up between

Billy's thighs, rubbing against the man's balls and the bottom of his cock.

Rourke and Billy had sat like this before, but usually it involved a lot of kissing and no handcuffs. And, while Rourke might have used his fingers on Billy's tight entrance, he'd never used his cock. That was about to change.

Rourke grabbed the condom and tore it open. He scooted Billy back far enough that he could roll the condom down his aching cock. Once that was done, he moved Billy back into place.

He grabbed the bottle of lube and poured some over his fingers then dropped the bottle back onto the bed. Rourke watched Billy's face carefully as he reached around his slim form and started pressing his fingers into the man.

Billy's face flushed, his eyes dropping partially closed. Rourke could feel the man's thighs tense against him. He knew he wasn't hurting Billy. They'd done this before on more than one occasion, and Billy always seemed to enjoy it. This time should be no different.

"Are you ready for this, baby?" Rourke asked as he worked his fingers in Billy's ass.

Billy sucked in his lower lip and nodded.

"Let me hear you say it."

"Please," Billy groaned as Rourke pushed in another finger and moved it around.

"Please what, baby?"

Rourke could feel the air in his lungs starting to move in and out of his chest more rapidly with each breath. Watching Billy become aroused was more exciting than seeing the man in handcuffs, and that surprised Rourke from the very beginning.

"Please...please..."

"Say it, baby," Rourke said as he watched Billy's eyelids flutter. "Tell me what you want."

Billy was really naive about some things. Rourke wasn't sure the man even knew more than a few swear words, even if he'd heard them. While it wouldn't be good in front of his family, Rourke was bound and determined to dirty up Billy's mouth in the bedroom. And he wanted to hear Billy ask for what he wanted.

"I want you to fuck me," Billy cried out.

That was all Rourke needed to hear. He pulled his fingers free from Billy's ass and grabbed the man's hips, lifting him into the air until he felt the head of his cock caught on the puckered hole of Billy's ass.

Rourke kept his eyes locked with Billy's as he slowly lowered the man down on his cock, one inch at a time. The feeling of his cock sinking into Billy's silken depths was exquisite, but not nearly as much as the look of wonder on Billy's flushed face.

When Billy finally rested fully against him, Rourke reached up and gripped the back of his neck, pulling Billy forward until their lips were a mere breath apart. "I'm in you now, baby. I'm never leaving."

Billy's breath hitched. Rourke could feel Billy's hands clenched against the nape of his neck. "Ne-never?"

"Nope." Rourke licked at Billy's lips with his tongue until he heard him groan. "You're my legend, Billy Thornton, and I'm keeping you."

Billy's entire body shuddered. Rourke had just a split second to grin before Billy attacked him. Their lips smashed together, Billy's arms tightening around Rourke's neck. Rourke kissed Billy back, their tongues brushing against each other in a maelstrom of passion.

He grabbed Billy's hips and lifted him up before bringing him back down again. Billy cried out against his lips. Rourke winced when Billy's fingers curled into his hair and pulled. Billy seemed to go wild. Every movement, every touch of his tongue or body was sensuous. Rourke just hoped Billy never learned how arousing it was to him. Billy could do him in.

Rourke tore his mouth away from Billy's when the lack of air started to become a concern. Breathing didn't seem to get any easier when he looked at Billy. Every bit of lust and desire the man felt was shining on his face. The man didn't hide any of it.

Rourke continued to move Billy up and down on his cock. The man's tight inner muscles gripped his cock like they didn't want him to leave. It was almost more pleasure than Rourke could handle. He knew it wouldn't be long before he exploded inside the man.

"Is this what you wanted, baby?"

"Wa-wanted to belong to you."

"You do, baby," Rourke whispered. "You will always belong to me."

Billy's head fell back on his shoulders, and small little cries came from his lips. Each sweet sound was exquisite to Rourke. He grabbed Billy around the waist and rolled them both on the mattress until he hovered over the top of the man.

Billy looked so wide eyed that Rourke couldn't help but grin. He grabbed Billy's arms and pulled them from around his neck, pushing them down onto the mattress over Billy's head. It took just a moment to hook the cuffs on the eyehook welded into the headboard.

Rourke sat back, lifting Billy's legs with his arms. He moved forward, reseating his cock in Billy's ass. He started moving, thrusting into Billy over and over again. "You're so fucking tight, baby," Rourke groaned. "You feel so good."

"Yes."

"I'm going to fuck you until we both pass out."

"Okay."

Rourke grinned at Billy's one-word answers. "Do you like that idea, baby? Do you want me to fuck you until you pass out?"

"Yes."

Rourke dropped one of Billy's legs so that he could reach up and grab the man's cock. He started stroking Billy's thick erection as he thrust into him. Drops of pre-cum dribbled down the sides of Billy's cock.

"Tell me what you want, baby," Rourke ordered.

"Fuck me."

"I am fucking you, baby."

Billy suddenly grinned, which surprised Rourke. "Fuck me harder."

Rourke growled and increased the pace of his thrusts. Billy's mouth dropped open. He started to pant heavily and tremble. His arms stiffened, his fingers tightening around the wrought iron headboard.

"Come for me, baby," Rourke demanded. "Come on my cock."

Billy's body arched into the air. A low cry filled the room as he came. Rourke's hand became slicker as cum shot out of Billy's cock. Silken muscles tightened around Rourke's cock, drawing a deep groan from him.

Rourke stroked Billy a few more times then dropped the man's cock and grabbed his leg again. He hooked Billy's feet over his shoulders then planted his hands in the mattress on either side of Billy's body.

Rourke pressed his lips together as he started pounding into Billy. The waves of ecstasy throbbed through him with every thrust. Fire burned through him, heating him from the inside out until he combusted into a ball of flames.

The sudden rattling of the handcuffs around Billy's hands drew Rourke's eyes upward. His lungs seemed unable to draw in any air. Billy was shaking the handcuffs, reminding Rourke that the man was under his mercy.

Rourke couldn't control his outcry of delight as his orgasm suddenly ripped through him. He stiffened. His cock throbbed and spilled inside of Billy's tight ass. A deep feeling of peace and contentment entered Rourke as he dropped Billy's legs and moved down over him.

He gently kissed Billy's swollen lips then looked into his deep blue eyes. "Are you okay? I didn't hurt you at all, did I?"

"No," Billy whispered.

Rourke smiled. "Good."

Billy rattled the cuffs again. "Can I have my hands?"

Rourke frowned. "That's not what you were asking before, was it?"

"No." Billy chuckled. "I was reminding you that I was handcuffed and displayed for your pleasure."

"Our pleasure," Rourke reminded Billy. He reached up and unlocked the handcuffs then watched Billy rub his wrists as he brought them back down. "Do they hurt?"

"Rourke."

"Just asking."

"I'm not going to break."

"You might."

Billy snorted and rolled his eyes. "If Clem can't break me, you can't either."

"Hey!" Rourke tapped the tip of Billy's nose. "Clem has no business in our bed."

"Our bed?"

Rourke could hear the uncertainty in Billy's voice. He could see it in his blue eyes. Billy was unsure of them, and he knew he needed to fix that. He gently pulled away from Billy and rolled to the side of the bed.

"Hold that thought," he said as he walked away.

He made a quick trip to the bathroom to clean up and brought back a wet washcloth. After wiping Billy down, Rourke tossed the washcloth to the floor then climbed back into bed beside Billy. He wrapped his arms around Billy and drew him closer.

"I told you that you were my legend, baby, and I meant it. That means I'm keeping you. So, yes, this is *our* bed if you want it to be."

"There's that word again, legend. What does it mean?"

"There's an old Blaecleah legend that says each Blaecleah will have one person that is meant only for them. And they will love this person for the rest of their lives. There will be no other for them." Rourke smiled and tightened his arms around Billy. "I knew the second I kissed you that you were it for me. I'll never love another, just you."

Rourke knew he was putting everything he felt out there on the line for Billy, but he knew the man needed more than the usual words. He needed to know Rourke meant everything he said, maybe more than the average person.

He knew he risked rejection from Billy, but he didn't think he'd get it. He knew Billy cared for him. He just didn't know if Billy cared for him enough to stick around. Billy had a lot to be scared of. Rourke wanted to be the one to protect him and give him a safe place to be.

When Billy didn't answer right away, Rourke began to grow concerned. He leaned back and peered down at Billy. When he spotted tears trailing down the man's face, he grew even more worried.

"Billy?"

Billy sniffed and wiped away at the tears on his cheek as he smiled. "I guess we should have kissed earlier then."

Chapter 9

"Rourke, Billy," Ma's voice called through the door as she knocked on it a few minutes later, "Sheriff Riley is here. He'd like to speak with both of you."

"The sheriff?" Billy's panic was immediate and nearly paralyzing. "I haven't done anything, Rourke, I swear. I haven't even left the ranch in days, and I've been with you nearly every second of every day."

"Baby, calm down." Rourke patted Billy's shoulder. "Sheriff Riley could just be here to talk to us about the barn. It doesn't mean he's here for you."

"Yeah, right, the barn." Billy still didn't believe it. If the sheriff was here, something was wrong, and Billy was terrified that he was about to lose everything he'd gained in the last week, hell, in the last hour.

Unless he was mistaken, and he could very well be, Rourke was keeping him forever. He had even declared his love. Maybe Billy wanted it so much that he had simply dreamed it or heard what he wanted to hear. Maybe he was wrong.

"Rourke." Billy curled his hands into the edge of the sheet and watched Rourke dress. "Did you mean it?"

"Mean what, baby?" Rourke asked as he started to pull a cotton shirt over his head.

"Th-that you're keeping me?" Billy whispered.

"What?" Rourke yanked the shirt down and turned to look at Billy. "Baby, what are you talking about?"

Billy knew it. He knew it was too good to be true. He tried to act nonchalant as he moved to the opposite side of the bed from Rourke. It wasn't easy when his whole body felt weighed down by his breaking heart. Rourke didn't want him.

"It weren't nothing."

"Baby, what are you going on about?"

Billy pressed his lips together, more to keep the sobs at bay than in defiance of Rourke's questions. He started to search the floor for his clothes, wanting nothing more than to get dressed and run.

"Baby, I can't understand you when you whisper like that."

Billy suddenly found himself surrounded by Rourke's arms. He tried not to struggle away because he was pretty sure this was the last time he'd feel like this. But when Rourke's hand gripped his chin and lifted his head, Billy couldn't help trying to pull away.

"Baby, what is wrong?"

"Nothing."

"You have got to stop whispering, baby."

"Nothing, okay?" Billy said, louder. "Nothing is wrong."

"You're lying, baby."

Billy squeezed his eyes shut. He really hated it that Rourke could read him so well. He couldn't hide anything from the man. Just once Billy wanted to get out of a situation with his dignity intact.

"Please let me go." Billy made sure that his voice was loud and firm this time. Rourke's arms immediately fell away from him, but the man's hands gripped Billy's face.

"Baby, you have got to tell me what has you so upset. I can't fix it if you don't tell me."

"You can't fix this."

"I don't even know what *this* is."

"It doesn't matter."

"It obviously does, baby, or you wouldn't be coming apart at the seams." Rourke frowned. "Is it the sheriff? Is that what's upset you?"

Billy nodded. He was worried about the sheriff, but that wasn't what upset him so much. He just wasn't going to tell Rourke that. Billy refused to beg for something that wasn't freely given, not matter how much he wanted it.

"Oh, baby," Rourke said as he wrapped Billy up in his arms again. "The sheriff can't do anything to you. You're mine now, baby, remember? That means the entire Blaecleah family is on your side."

"What?"

Rourke chuckled. "You're mumbling again, baby."

"What?" Billy asked, louder.

"You, my little love, are mine forever, remember? You're my legend, and I'm keeping you. That means that every member of my family and I will do everything within our power to keep you safe, even from the sheriff."

"You're keeping me?"

"I'm keeping you," Rourke repeated.

"Forever?"

"Yes, baby, I'm keeping you forever."

Billy slumped against Rourke as his heart started beating again. Forever, Rourke was keeping him forever. He pressed his face against Rourke's shirt as the tears in his eyes threatened to spill over.

"Hey, look at me." Rourke nudged Billy's face up. "I know you haven't had a lot of good things in your life, but I want to change that. I want to give you the world."

"I just want you."

Rourke smiled and gave Billy a quick kiss on the lips. "You have me."

Billy jumped when there was another sudden knock on the bedroom door. "Rourke? Billy?" Ma called out. "The sheriff is waiting."

"This isn't going to go well, Rourke," Billy said as he stepped away from Rourke. He rubbed his hands up and down his arms to ward off the sudden chill he felt. "I can feel it in my bones."

"Let's not buy trouble, baby. We'll just go out and see what the sheriff wants and go from there."

Billy knew it wouldn't be that easy. He'd dealt with the sheriff before. Granted, Sheriff Riley was better than Sheriff Miller, who retired a few months ago. Sheriff Riley didn't try to arrest Billy on sight. Sheriff Miller seemed to have it out for him. Billy had been ecstatic when Sheriff Miller retired. He just didn't know much about the new sheriff.

"You better get dressed, baby."

Dressed, right. Billy searched around until he found his clothes and quickly pulled them on. Despite the warmth in the room, he still felt chilled. "Rourke, do you have a long-sleeved shirt I can borrow?"

"Sure, baby, look in the closet. There should be something in there."

Billy searched the closet until he found one of Rourke's smaller flannel shirts. The larger ones made him look like he was wearing a dress. He pulled it on and buttoned it up, laughing quietly to himself when he had to roll up the sleeves. At least it didn't hang down to his knees.

"Well, how do I look?" Billy asked as he held his hands out to his sides.

"Gorgeous." Rourke grinned.

"You think I look gorgeous?" Billy frowned. "Are you feeling all right?"

Rourke burst out laughing, which was a good look on the man and made Billy feel better, but he still thought the man was a little off. Billy wasn't gorgeous, and he knew it. He might be able to pass for cute, if he was lucky.

"Okay, I guess that's another thing we need to work on."

"What?"

"Your self-esteem, baby. You need to learn how special you are."

"I…you…" Billy blinked rapidly. The shirt collar around his neck suddenly felt tighter, and he reached up to run his finger over it, pulling it away from his throat. "You're nuts."

"No, and I'll prove it to you as soon as we get done talking with the sheriff."

"Handcuffs again?" Billy wiggled his eyebrows.

"I've created a monster." Rourke chuckled.

Billy smiled as he followed Rourke out of the bedroom, but that smile fell from his lips the moment he stepped out onto the porch and saw his father standing next to the sheriff's car.

"What can we help you with, sheriff?" Rourke asked.

Billy edged his way closer to Rourke, stepping slightly behind him. His father wasn't paying any attention to him, which wasn't unusual. He never paid Billy any attention.

"Billy, can you come down here by me, please?"

"Me?"

The sheriff nodded.

Billy just knew the sheriff was there for him. He stepped out from behind Rourke and started down the porch steps when Rourke grabbed his arm, stopping him.

"What's this all about, sheriff?"

"Rourke, I've had a report that you're holding Billy Thornton here against his will."

"Excuse me?"

The sheriff gestured over his shoulder to Ira Thornton. "Ira filed a report with my office this morning. He says you're holding Billy here against his will."

Billy started shaking his head. "No, that's not true."

"Are you here of your own free will, Billy?"

"Yes." He wasn't going to let his father destroy the happiness he'd found with Rourke and the rest of the Blaecleah family. "I'm here because I want to be here."

"Well." The sheriff hooked his thumbs in his belt buckle. "I suppose that's good enough for me."

Billy started to breathe a sigh of relief until Ira stomped across the yard. He cringed, quickly stepping back up the steps.

"You're just going to take his word for it?" Ira shouted.

"Yeah, pretty much," the sheriff replied.

"It's obvious that Billy is under duress."

Billy flinched when his father started waving his hands around wildly in the air. He didn't even know his father knew what the word *duress* meant.

"Look at him!" Ira shouted. "He's terrified. He's not going to answer truthfully with the whole Blaecleah family standing there surrounding him. Who knows what they threatened him with?"

Billy was terrified, but not from any one of the Blaecleah family. He was terrified of the angry glint in his father's eyes. Ira Thornton looked pissed. Billy didn't even understand why his father was there.

"Billy," the sheriff said, "why don't you come down here and talk with me?"

"I don't want to."

"Billy."

Billy shook his head frantically. He didn't mind talking with the sheriff, well, not much anyway. But he wasn't about to take a step closer to his father. Clem was off his rocker, but he learned it from their father.

"Baby, you have to."

Billy looked up at Rourke, silently pleading with him.

"Sorry, baby, but the only way to clear this up is to talk with the sheriff."

Billy's shoulders slumped in defeat, and he slowly made his way down the steps to stand in front of the sheriff. "What do you want to know?" he asked softly.

"Has Rourke, or any of the Blaecleah family, held you here or anywhere else against your will?"

"No."

"Have they kept you from leaving?"

"No."

"Do you want to be here?"

"Yes."

"That's good enough for me."

Billy breathed a sigh of relief and turned to go back up the stairs when Ira started shouting again. Billy's heart sank with each word he spoke.

"He's lying!" Ira yelled. "Look at his wrists. It's clear that they've been abusing him. He's too scared to go against them."

Billy hid his hands behind his back. He started stepping back when the sheriff turned to look at him, one of his blond eyebrows arched.

"Billy?"

Billy shook his head and took another step back.

"Billy, I need to see your wrists." The sheriff held out his hands.

Billy glanced up at Rourke, unsure of what to do. Rourke nodded. Billy reluctantly turned back to the sheriff and held out his hands. The sheriff grabbed his hands, turning them over then back again as he looked at the slight reddening around Billy's wrists.

"How'd this happen, Billy?"

"I...uh..." Billy looked up at Rourke even as he felt his face flush with embarrassment. He could see all of the other Blaecleah family members staring at him. Rourke just crossed his arms over his chest as if he was waiting for something. Billy just didn't know what.

Should he be truthful and tell the sheriff how he got the red marks or lie and hide it from everyone? Using handcuffs during sex was a pretty private thing. Billy didn't know if Rourke wanted him to admit that they did it.

"Billy, I asked you a question," the sheriff said. "I need an answer. How did you get these red marks on your wrists?"

"Ha-handcuffs," Billy whispered, hoping only the sheriff would hear him.

"Handcuffs?"

Billy nodded.

"And who put the handcuffs on you, Billy?"

Billy looked up at Rourke again, seeking guidance, but the man didn't move a muscle, not even a raising of his eyebrow. Billy knew he was on his own with this question. He looked back at the sheriff to find the man watching him intently.

"Rourke."

"Rourke handcuffed you?"

"Yes, but—"

"See?" Ira shouted. "I told you they were abusing Billy."

"No, that's not—"

"What else have they done to you, Billy?" Ira yelled as he stalked closer. "They're perverts, every last one of them. They need to be locked up, sheriff."

"No, you don't understand," Billy said quickly. He tried to back away, but the sheriff still had a hold of his wrists. "Please, you don't—"

"Are you hurt anywhere else, Billy?" the sheriff asked.

Billy shook his head. "No, not exactly, but I—"

"Not exactly?" The sheriff started looking Billy over. "What do you mean *not exactly?*"

"I want Rourke Blaecleah arrested for kidnapping and assault, sheriff. There's no telling what other perverted things he's done to my son."

Billy's mouth dropped open as his father walked over to stand a few feet away. His father never cared one wit about him, not since he was in diapers, and maybe not even then. Billy didn't understand why he was making an issue of things now.

"No, this is wrong," Billy said quickly. "I wasn't—"

Before Billy could finish what he was saying, his father jumped over and grabbed him. Billy cried out and tried to break free of his father's grasp. Before he could, Ira pulled up the back of his shirt and swung him around so his back was to the sheriff.

"Look what they did to him!"

Billy pulled away from his father and tried to run up the stairs only to hit a wall of muscles. Frightened and feeling out of control, Billy cried out and shrank back, not realizing it was Rourke holding him until the man's arms closed around him.

"Rourke, I'm afraid I'm going to have to take you in for questioning," the sheriff said. Billy heard the rattling of metal, and a moment later, Rourke lifted his arms and stepped away.

"No!" Billy cried out when he saw the handcuffs on Rourke's wrists. "You don't understand."

"I'm sure everything can be explained down at the sheriff's office, Billy," the sheriff said as he started to lead Rourke away.

Billy looked up at the other members of the Blaecleah family only to find them just standing there, watching the sheriff lead Rourke away. He didn't understand why they weren't explaining things to the sheriff.

"Wait, please," Billy cried out as he ran after the sheriff and Rourke. "I don't want Rourke arrested."

"Billy—" the sheriff began, only to be interrupted by Ira.

"No, you're absolutely correct, Billy."

Billy swung around to see his father calmly walking toward him, a strange smile on his face. He knew his father was up to something. He just didn't know what it was. And he was afraid to find out.

"I understand that you're afraid, Billy," Ira said as he wrapped his arm around Billy's shoulders. Billy was pretty sure that anyone looking would only see a father consoling his son. They wouldn't see the fear that was overwhelming Billy. "I think you have a right to be. It's obvious that the Blaecleah family has abused you horribly."

Billy's mouth dropped open. His father was just as crazy as Clem.

"Sheriff, my son may be too afraid to testify against anyone in the Blaecleah family, especially Rourke. As such, I would be willing to drop the charges if the entire Blaecleah family swears that they will have no further contact with Billy."

"What?" Billy whispered, his heart dropping.

"Otherwise, I will have to ask that charges of kidnapping and assault be filed against Rourke and his entire family. It's the only way to keep my son safe."

Billy's life was going up in flames right before his eyes. "Rourke!"

"It's okay, baby, we'll get this all worked out down at the sheriff's office."

"Baby!" Ira shouted. Billy winced when his father's hands tightened on him. "You're calling him *baby*? What else have you done to my son? Did you rape him, too?"

Billy inhaled sharply when Rourke pulled away from the sheriff and lunged at Ira. He quickly stepped between them, pushing against Rourke's chest. "No, don't," Billy whispered quickly. "You know what will happen if you attack my father."

"This isn't over, Ira!" Rourke growled. His jaw clenched, but he settled back. A moment later, the sheriff pulled Rourke away and tried to lead him to the car again.

"You heard that, sheriff? He's threatening me."

"I heard," the sheriff admitted grudgingly.

Billy twisted his fingers together as he watched the sheriff take Rourke away. This was wrong, all wrong. And no one seemed to be doing anything about it. No one was saying anything. Everyone in the Blaecleah family knew who had abused Billy. Why weren't they saying anything?

"Sheriff." Billy swallowed hard and tried to draw up his courage when the sheriff stopped walking Rourke to his car and turned to look at him. "If I go home with my father, will you let Rourke go?"

"Billy, no!" Rourke shouted. He started to struggle against the sheriff's grasp.

"I…I can't let you go to jail."

"Billy, it will be okay," Rourke said. "Just let the sheriff do his job."

"Sheriff, will you let Rourke go if I go home with my father?"

"Do you or your father plan to press charges against him?" the sheriff asked.

"No." Billy shook his head.

"Then I don't see a problem."

"Billy, you can't do this!" Rourke snapped. "Think. You know what will happen if you go home."

Billy nodded. He did know what would happen, but he couldn't let anything happen to Rourke. He'd spent too many years trying to protect the man, and he couldn't stop now. It was kind of ingrained in him.

Billy bit his lip then turned to look up at the people standing on the porch. "Would you hold him? He's going to get upset, and I don't want to see him get hurt."

Da, Ma, and all of the Blaecleah brothers nodded. Billy turned back to see Rourke glaring at him. He fidgeted, tugging on the hem of the shirt he'd borrowed from Rourke and watched as Lachlan, Quaid, and Seamus all stepped down from the porch and walked over to surround Rourke. Billy waited until they had a good hold of Rourke's arms before walking over to stand in front of him.

"I'm sorry," Billy whispered.

"Baby, don't do this."

"I have to." Billy smiled through the tears he could feel beginning to glisten in his eyes. He reached up and cradled the side of Rourke's face in his hand. "You were always my special someone."

Chapter 10

Rourke watched with dumbfounded disbelief as Billy walked away with his father and climbed into the back of the man's truck. He could see the fear on Billy's face as he sat in the bed of the truck as it drove away. He knew where Billy was headed just as much as Billy did, and he didn't know why no one had stopped the man.

The moment he felt the hands holding him loosen, Rourke yanked away from his brothers. He pressed his lips together to keep from shouting at his family and held his hands out to the sheriff, waiting for the man to take the handcuffs off.

Once they were off and the sheriff had stepped back, Rourke turned to glare at each member of his family. He didn't leave the sheriff out of his intense, angry stare either. He blamed each and every one of them for putting Billy in danger.

"What is wrong with all of you?" he asked, his tone low and menacing. "You know what will happen to Billy when Clem gets a hold of him. How could you let Billy leave?"

"Billy made his choice, Rourke," Da said. "You have to respect it."

"That wasn't a choice," Rourke shouted as he waved his hand toward the driveway. "That was sheer and utter terror."

"Rourke—"

"You know what Clem did to him the last time." Rourke clenched his fists as more anger filled him, along with a healthy dose of fear for Billy. "Billy will be lucky to walk away with his life this time."

"Rourke, what are you talking about?" the sheriff asked.

Rourke swung around to glare at the man. He held him just as responsible as his family. "I didn't beat Billy. Clem did. He's been doing it for years."

"Then why didn't he say something to me?"

"Because he's scared," Rourke said. "The one time he tried to report things to Sheriff Miller, the man laughed at Billy and sent him home, where he received another beating for telling what Clem had done to him. He has no reason to trust you."

Sheriff Riley grimaced. "Yes, that does kind of make sense. I've only been in office for a few months, but already I've had a lot of reports of Sheriff Miller's activities. He seems to have his own brand of justice."

"He should have protected Billy."

"That's assuming he knew exactly what was going on with Billy. I'm still not sure."

"It doesn't matter," Rourke snapped. "He should have at least investigated it when Billy reported what Clem was doing."

"You have to admit that Billy has somewhat of a reputation, Rourke. Sheriff Miller might not have believed him."

"And that's supposed to make a difference?" Rourke rubbed the back of his neck with his hand. His muscles were so tense they ached. He couldn't stop thinking about what Billy might be going through. "Billy needed help, and no one listened to him."

"That still doesn't explain the handcuffs, Rourke."

Rourke rolled his eyes. "So, I'm kinky and like to play around with handcuffs. Sue me."

"You're saying that Billy willingly let you handcuff him?"

"Yes, and Billy would tell you the same thing if he were standing here. He tried to tell you when he was here, and you wouldn't listen to him."

"And the marks on his back?" the sheriff asked. "Was that part of your play, too?"

"No." Rourke chuckled sadly. "I told you, that was all Clem."

"Clem?"

"A few nights ago, Billy showed up here all beat up. Clem had whipped Billy until he was nothing but a bloody mess. Billy's been here ever since."

"Didn't he leave a note on your windshield, Rourke?" Seamus asked.

"Yeah." Rourke took off running, leaping up the steps and into the house. He ran into his bedroom and started searching for the note. By the time he found it sitting on the floor just under the edge of his bed, the room looked like a tornado had ripped through it. Rourke didn't care. He grabbed the note and ran back outside.

Jumping down the steps, Rourke held the note out to the sheriff. "The night Billy got here he was putting this under my windshield wiper."

"Beware of Clem. He means you harm," the sheriff read out loud then looked up at Rourke. "He left this on your windshield?"

Rourke nodded.

"Did he say why?"

"From what I understand, Billy has been protecting me for years."

"Protecting you?"

"Clem hates me and my entire family. He's hated us for years. Billy tried to keep Clem from hurting us."

"How?"

Rourke frowned. "Billy has been giving Clem someone else to train his anger on, himself."

"Damn it, Rourke." The sheriff clenched his hand around the note and glanced around. "Do you know what you're saying?"

"Yes, I'm saying that all of you let Billy walk out of here and sent him into hell."

"I didn't have any other choice, Rourke. Billy is an adult. If he wanted to leave, I had to let him."

Rourke felt like stomping his foot in frustration. No one seemed to be getting the danger Billy was in. "What part of this aren't you getting? Billy didn't *want* to leave. He thought he was protecting me, and Billy would do anything to protect me."

"From who?" the sheriff asked. "Clem wasn't even here. Hell, none of my deputies can even find the man. Who was Billy protecting you from?"

"You might not be able to find him, but Clem is around somewhere. He's obsessed with Billy. He won't go far."

"Obsessed?"

Rourke sighed. "The night Clem whipped Billy, he did it because he saw us kiss. Later, Clem attacked us in the woods and tried to strangle Billy. He kept going on about Billy belonging to him."

"He tried to kill Billy?" the sheriff asked. "Why didn't you call me and report it?"

"It's only been a couple of days, sheriff," Da said as he walked down the steps and over to stand next to Rourke. "We were going to call you, but it seemed more important to give Billy time to heal. He was in pretty bad shape."

"You should have called me." The sheriff folded the note up and slid it into his pocket. "I can't very well protect the citizens of this town if I don't know they are in danger."

"Well, now you know Billy is in danger," Rourke snapped as he started toward the sheriff's vehicle. "Let's go protect him."

"Uh, Rourke," Lachlan said. Rourke looked over to see his brother stiffen and point. "I think it's too late for that."

Rourke whipped around to see what Lachlan was talking about and nearly collapsed on the ground as fear filled every cell in his body. Billy was running through the field between the ranch and the woods like his life depended on it.

And it might. Clem was chasing after Billy as fast as he could. Rourke took off running. He could hear people shouting behind him, but all he cared about was reaching Billy. His heart stuttered in his chest when he saw Clem raise a gun in his hand and a loud bang filled the air.

Billy went down, his body hidden by the tall grass. Rourke tried to run faster, to reach Billy before Clem did. Loud shouts and the sound of feet pounding on the ground were drowned out by the pounding in Rourke's head as Billy suddenly jumped up and started running again.

"Billy!" Rourke yelled as loud as he could as he ran.

Billy's head came up and looked in his direction. Even with the distance between them, Rourke could see the relief on Billy's face as the man altered his path and started running toward him.

Rourke didn't stop running until Billy barreled into him. He wrapped his arm around Billy and, in one move, turned them both and started running back the way he came. He kept his arm around Billy's waist, helping him along and trying to put himself between Billy and Clem.

Rourke could hear Clem firing his gun. One bullet whizzed so close to his head that he felt the disturbance in the air as it passed. Rourke was terrified that Billy would be hit, but he just kept running, pushing Billy ahead of him.

"Get down!" the sheriff shouted.

Rourke dropped to the ground immediately, taking Billy with him. He heard Billy grunt as they hit the ground but didn't have time to stop and ask if he was okay. Instead, he moved up and covered Billy's body with his own.

Shots fired over his head, making Rourke's ears ring. He closed his eyes and held on to Billy, burying his face in the man's hair as he prayed the sheriff's aim was better than Clem's.

"Love you, baby," he whispered into Billy's ear. If they were going to die, he wanted his words to be the last Billy ever heard.

Billy turned his head and looked back over his shoulder. Rourke could see the fear in Billy's deep blue eyes. They both knew the danger they were in. Still, a small smile moved over Billy's lips.

"Love you, Rourke," he murmured, "always have, always will."

Billy's body jerked when a sudden loud shot rang out overhead. Rourke tightened his arms around the man and hunched over him a little more, trying to make sure that his body covered all of Billy's.

Rourke cringed when he heard a soft sob come from the man beneath him. Billy was terrified. If Rourke didn't feel the need to protect Billy he would jump up and confront Clem, tear the man limb from limb for what he was doing to the man he loved.

"Rourke, you can get up now."

Rourke glanced over his shoulder to see his Da standing over the top of him. Lachlan and Seamus stood right behind him. "Clem?"

Da gestured behind Rourke. "The sheriff shot him. I don't think he's dead, but he is wounded."

Rourke pushed himself up a little and looked behind him. Sure enough, the sheriff was handcuffing Clem's hands behind his back. Clem was on his feet, but a stain of red was blooming across his shoulder.

Rourke slowly climbed to his feet then reached back down for Billy. "It's safe to get up now, baby. The sheriff has your brother in custody."

Billy's hand trembled as he laid it in Rourke's and stood to his feet. His face was pale and smeared with dirt, and Rourke didn't think he ever looked better. He was alive, and that was all that mattered to Rourke.

Billy immediately moved into the curve of Rourke's body. Rourke wrapped both arms around Billy and pulled him as close as two people could get without being in the same skin. He planted kiss after kiss on the top of Billy's head.

"Damn, baby," Rourke whispered. "I thought I'd lost you."

"I thought you had, too," Billy replied. "Clem was waiting for us at the end of the driveway."

"He was waiting for you?"

Billy nodded. "My father stopped the truck at the end of the driveway and Clem got in. The truck started moving again before I could escape, so I had to wait until my father slowed down to turn into the driveway. I jumped out of the back, but Clem saw me and started after me."

"So, you came here?"

Billy was smiling by the time he tilted his head back. "I knew you'd be waiting for me."

"Actually." Rourke chuckled. "I was chewing everyone out for letting you leave."

"Well, that was stupid. I had to leave."

"No." Rourke shook his head. "You didn't."

"The sheriff was going to arrest you. I couldn't let that happen."

"Baby, he just wanted to question me. We could have worked this all out by simply talking with him down at the sheriff's office."

"Yeah, I don't think so. Once you're in handcuffs, it's hard to get out of them."

"You don't seem to mind."

Rourke laughed and hugged Billy as the man's face flushed red. The sheriff was leading the handcuffed and injured Clem to his police car. Billy was safe, his family was safe, and the danger was being locked away. Rourke felt almost giddy with relief.

"Rourke," the sheriff called out, "I'm going to need a statement from you and Billy."

Billy groaned and buried his face in Rourke's shirt.

"Come on, baby, let's go talk with the sheriff, and then we can talk about reasons why you shouldn't leave."

"I didn't want to leave, Rourke. I had to." Billy's head came up, and his hands started rubbing against Rourke's chest. "I had to keep you safe."

Rourke wanted to growl in frustration and shout with joy all at the same time. Billy was so protective of him, and Rourke loved that about the man, but he was protective at his own expense. And Rourke couldn't allow that.

"Baby," Rourke began as he stroked his hand down the side of Billy's face, "there are other ways to keep me safe, to keep us both safe. You don't always have to put yourself in danger."

"I don't know…" Billy shrugged. "I don't know any other way to do it."

The corner of Rourke's mouth curved up. "Then we'll just have to teach you. We can start by going to talk to the sheriff. He's not like Sheriff Miller, baby. Riley will listen to you. He believes that you're a good guy, and so do I."

"Really?"

"I do." Rourke wrapped his arm around Billy's waist and began leading him toward the sheriff. He could see his family standing around at the bottom of the porch steps, talking. After being shot at, it felt good to see them all standing there safe.

"Billy, son, would you like some tea?" Ma asked the moment they stepped up to the small group of people. "I think this occasion calls for some tea."

"That would be wonderful, Mrs. Blaecleah."

Rourke saw a lot of food in their future.

"Ma." Ma shook her finger at Billy. "If you plan on sticking around here, you'd better start calling me Ma."

"Yes, ma'am."

Rourke chuckled at the near panicked look on Billy's face. Billy learned quickly though. "Billy and I will come inside for that tea in just a few minutes, Ma. We need to talk to the sheriff first."

"That's fine. You just see that that young man of yours doesn't stay out here too long. He's still healing from his injuries. He needs his rest."

"Yes, ma'am."

Rourke smiled as he watched his ma walk up the steps and into the house. He knew Billy still needed rest, and he had every intention of getting the man back into bed as soon as he could. The *rest* would come after that, long after that.

"Billy, I need to ask you some questions, and you may find them hard to answer, but it's important that you're truthful with me."

Rourke tensed at his Da's words. He pulled Billy back into the curve of his body, protecting him as best as he could.

"As much as it pains me to say so, we know your brother is a danger to you."

"Yes, sir," Billy murmured.

"I can't allow him here anymore, Billy. I can't let him hurt you or my sons anymore. Do you understand that?"

Billy's body stiffened for a moment then sort of slumped against Rourke. "Do you want me to leave?"

"Oh, no, son, that's not what I mean at all," Da said quickly. "We told you that you were always welcome here, and that still holds true. I just want you to understand that I can't allow Clem to continue to hurt you or my sons anymore. It has to stop, Billy. And I believe you're the only one that can do it."

"What do you want me to do?"

"You need to press charges against Clem for what he did to you, Billy. It should never have happened in the first place, but it did, and now it's time to stop it. Clem doesn't have the right to hurt you."

"I know. I just…"

"Billy," Rourke said, "Da is right. It's time that this stopped. I'm sorry you're being put in a position where you have to go against your brother but—"

"I could care less about that," Billy said. "Clem hasn't been a brother to me in years. I just don't want anything I do coming back on any of you. Clem can hold a grudge for a very long time."

"What about your father, Billy?" Da asked. "Does he hold a grudge as well?"

"I don't know. If you had asked me that this morning before he arrived with the sheriff, I would have said no. My father has never really cared what I did as long as I stayed out of his hair. But now, I just don't know."

"Fair enough," Da said.

"I think you need to mention that to the sheriff as well, baby."

"I heard, Rourke."

Rourke turned to see the sheriff standing behind him. He nodded at the man. "What do we need to do to keep Billy safe from his family?"

"I'm not sure there is much I can do about Ira. Besides making false accusations, he hasn't done anything wrong."

"He's allowed Clem to beat on Billy," Rourke growled.

"Not something that can really be proven in a court of law, Rourke, no matter how much we may wish otherwise. We can take out a restraining order barring Ira from your property, but unless we have actual proof that he even knew what was happening to Billy, my hands are tied."

"Then do that."

"Rourke, you need to make sure that's what Billy wants," Da said. "No matter how we feel, Ira is still Billy's father."

"Baby?"

Billy turned to look at the sheriff. "If we had one of those restraining things, it would keep my father away from the Blaecleahs?"

"Here on the ranch, yes. Ira wouldn't be allowed to step foot on Blaecleah land. If he did, then I could put him in jail."

"As long as the Blaecleah family is protected, I'll do whatever you want."

"Baby, you have to stop trying to protect us."

Billy snorted and leaned back in Rourke's arms. "Yeah, like that's going to happen."

Chapter 11

"Mr. Blaecleah?"

"How many times have I told you, son, if you're going to be living here, you need to call me Da."

"Sorry, sir." It had been over three weeks since his brother was arrested by the sheriff and Billy took a restraining order out on his father. He still wasn't used to the acceptance he received from the Blaecleah family.

He expected acceptance from Rourke. They were working on a relationship together. They still had a few issues to work out, like the fact that Rourke insisted Billy didn't need to protect him. But Billy knew someone had to. Rourke took too many chances with his safety. He needed a keeper.

Billy knew he was the man for the job. As much as he knew Rourke wished he'd stop, Billy couldn't. He'd been doing it for years. It came as natural to him as breathing. Billy would die if anything happened to Rourke.

"So, what can I do for you, son?"

Bill took in a deep breath for courage then quickly blurted out what he wanted. "I was wondering if you had any odd jobs I could do around the ranch to earn some money."

Da frowned and stood up, setting the ropes in his hand down on the bench next to him. "You need some money, son?"

"Not much, I promise. I just—"

"Billy, if you need some money, all you have to do is ask." Da started to reach for the wallet in his back pocket.

Billy quickly raised his hand to stop him. "I'd prefer earning it if I could."

Da frowned and dropped his hand down to rest it on the bench. "What's this all about, Billy?"

Billy twisted his fingers together and looked down at them. The intensity of Da's eyes was too much for him to look at while he confessed his sins. "I've done a lot of bad things in the past, and I have some people to make it up to, people that I stole from. I think it's only right that I earn the money to pay them back."

Da was silent. Billy began to get worried that he'd let too much information out. Everyone in the Blaecleah family knew of Billy's past. They still seemed to accept him, but Billy wanted more than that. He wanted their approval as well.

When Da didn't answer right away, Billy grabbed the edge of his shirt and started twisting it around his fingers. He would be devastated if Da Blaecleah discovered how much he'd messed up before Rourke decided they belonged together. He'd been a royal screwup.

"I'm sure we can find something around here for you to do, Billy," Da finally said.

"I'll do anything, muck stalls, dig fence posts, stack hay bales." Billy shrugged. "I'm pretty good general labor."

Da nodded and picked the rope up again. "Why don't we start with you straightening up this tack room? It could use a good going over. Cleaning and organizing it kind of gets forgotten when we work the ranch all day long."

"Thank you." Billy immediately started straightening up the room.

"Does Rourke know about this, son?"

Billy froze then slowly glanced over his shoulder. "No, sir."

"Are you going to tell him?"

"I wasn't really planning on it."

"Do you think it's a good idea to hide things from Rourke? He's bound to notice you doing extra work around the ranch."

"Yeah, he would at that." Billy chuckled. Rourke seemed to watch Billy's every move. Billy knew it was because Rourke was concerned about him, and that gave him a warm feeling deep down inside. But it still felt a little strange when Rourke complained when Billy worked hard. He wasn't used to someone being concerned for him.

"So, don't you think you should tell him?"

Billy sighed and sat down on one of the wooden boxes stacked against the wall. He looked down at his hands again. "I don't want Rourke to be disappointed in me."

"Son." Da chuckled. "I don't think that's possible."

"I've done a lot of bad things in my life. If Rourke was ever to find out everything I've done, he'd be very disappointed in me."

"Billy, you did what you needed to do to survive."

"That's not an excuse."

"No, it's not. It's an explanation. And I don't believe that anyone has the right to pass judgment on you if they haven't lived your life. You did what you had to do in some horrible circumstances."

"It doesn't excuse what I did."

"Billy, did you ever intentionally hurt anyone?"

Billy's head snapped up. "No!"

"But you did steal and threaten people, didn't you?"

Billy glanced down at his hands again. He was ashamed of his actions. He had been ashamed when he did them. He just hadn't been able to stop from doing them. Despite what he knew everyone thought, he knew Clem would have been a lot worse if Billy hadn't stepped in.

Billy couldn't count the number of times he'd stepped up and threatened someone, intimidated them. From their point of view, Billy imagined he seemed like a monster. He just knew he had to place himself between them and Clem. It was better if Billy was threatening them than if Clem was.

The stealing he'd done was pretty much the same. Billy knew if he was the one doing the stealing then he could pick and choose what he took, making sure he never took anything important. Clem would have just taken everything.

"I did a lot of things," Billy murmured. "None of them I'm proud of."

"You protected Rourke for years and almost lost your life doing it. That's something to be proud of, Billy, and something I will always be grateful for. Rourke means the world to me and his ma. We'd be devastated if anything ever happened to him."

"Rourke means everything to me, too."

"Then you should tell him, son. Hiding things from Rourke is not the way to start off your life together."

Billy sighed deeply. "It's just so hard."

"Nothing good is ever easy, son. If it's hard enough for you to fight for, then it's worth it in the long run."

"I suppose I should tell him." Billy couldn't think of anything he wanted to do less than talk to Rourke and tell him about everything he'd done, but Da had a point. Billy didn't like lying to Rourke or keeping things from him.

"The tack room will be here when you get back."

Billy nodded and stood to his feet. As much as he wanted to see Rourke because the man had been working since early this morning, Billy kind of felt like he might be walking toward his doom.

He tracked Rourke down to one of the stalls inside the new barn. Rourke was brushing down one of the horses. Billy leaned against one of the posts in the barn and watched Rourke work. He could just sit and watch Rourke for hours. The man was breathtaking.

"I can hear you thinking, baby."

Billy chuckled and walked over to join Rourke. He rested his arms on the top of the half wall of the stall and leaned his chin on his fingers. "You look like you're having fun."

Rourke snorted. "Oh, yeah, brushing horses is what I live for."

"Oh, I don't know. I think it would be kind of soothing." Billy reached out and stroked his hand along the horse's soft hair. "He doesn't ask for much beyond food and a safe place to sleep, and small things like getting brushed make him happy."

"What about you, baby," Rourke asked as he set the brush down on the edge of the stall wall, "what makes you happy?"

Billy's answer was immediate. He knew it without even thinking about it. "You do."

Rourke smiled as he settled his arms down on the stall wall right next to Billy's and rested his chin on his own fingers. Their faces were a mere inch from each other. "So, what did you come in here to talk to me about, baby?"

"How do you know I wanted to talk to you?" Billy smirked. "Maybe I came in to talk to the horse."

"Well, then," Rourke said as he stepped back and waved to the horse, "have at it. I was hoping for something a little different, but if you feel the need to talk to my horse, by all means, go ahead."

Billy would have thought Rourke was mad by the tone of his words if he hadn't seen the sly grin on his face. "Actually, I do need to talk to you about something. I guess the horse can wait."

"What?"

"I asked your da if he had any odd jobs for me to do around the ranch so that I could earn some money."

"Baby, if you need money, all you have to do is ask. What's mine is yours."

"I know, but I need to earn this money myself. I did some real bad things when I was with Clem, and if I ever hope to be accepted by the people of Cade Creek then I have some atonement to make."

"Baby, if this—"

"Please understand, this is something that I need to do on my own."

Rourke looked at him for several intense moments then nodded his head. His hand gently patted Billy's. "I do understand, baby, but I also want you to understand where I'm coming from. If you need help, I want you to ask me. While you may need to do this on your own, you are not on your own."

"I know."

"I'll always stand by your side, Billy."

"Baby."

"You're just not ever going to let me forget, are you?" Rourke chuckled.

Billy grinned. "Nope."

"I suppose I can get used to it."

"You'd better. You started it."

"Speaking of starting things, I have something for you."

"Oh?" Billy watched Rourke reach into his back pocket and pull out his wallet. When he opened it up, he grabbed two pictures. One, he shoved back into its plastic holder. The other one he held out to Billy.

"Yours got ruined, so I thought I'd get you another one."

Billy's breath caught in his throat when he looked down at the picture Rourke handed him. It wasn't the same picture Billy had from before. This one was even better. It was a picture of Billy and Rourke together.

Billy was leaning back against Rourke's larger body. His eyes were closed as he tilted his face up into the sun. Rourke's arms were wrapped around him, and he was looking down at Billy's upturned face. Everything Rourke felt for Billy was shining in the smile on his face.

"Rourke," Billy whispered past the lump of tears forming in his throat.

"I wanted you to have something to hold on to, something you could look at every day, any time you wanted to, that proved to you that you belong here." Rourke tapped the picture with his finger. "There's a framed one in my dresser drawer. I thought we could put it on the bedroom wall until we move into our new house."

"We're moving?" Billy looked up at Rourke, thoughts of the picture leaving his head, to be replaced by the fear that he'd have to leave the ranch. The mere thought made his heart ache. He loved living here. He felt safe, accepted. He didn't want to move.

"There's this real nice plot of land over by the woods that holds some special memories for us. Ma and Da already said we could have it, and I thought it would make a wonderful place for our back porch."

"Special memories?"

"That's the first place we ever kissed, remember?"

Billy frowned. "And that's a special memory for you?"

"For us, baby, for us. It was the first time I saw you as something more than Billy Thornton the troublemaker. That one little kiss set us on a path that brought us where we are today. I'd say that was pretty special."

"So, you want to build a house there?"

"Can you think of a better place?" Rourke chuckled. "I'm even marking that tree so that the builders don't touch it."

"What tree?"

"That tree I had you against the first time we kissed, the first time you ever came for me."

Billy inhaled sharply, his face burning.

"You didn't think I knew about that, did you?"

Billy's skin might have been flushed with embarrassment, but the heated look Rourke sent over his body burned him alive and made him ache.

"Well." Billy swallowed hard. "You did say I was a hot little piece."

"You are, but you're my hot little piece."

Billy opened his mouth to argue with Rourke. He wasn't prepared for the tongue that invaded his mouth instead. But he didn't argue. Kissing Rourke was like having a prelude to what heaven was like.

Rourke's lips roamed over Billy's. His tongue licked Billy's lips then brushed against Billy's tongue before delving inside to explore.

Billy's pulse went from normal to hyperactive in the blink of an eye, or the lick of a tongue. Billy moaned and leaned into the kiss, wanting more.

"Okay, I'll be your hot little piece," Billy whispered when Rourke finally pulled away. He would have agreed to anything for one of Rourke's kisses, and he knew it.

Rourke chuckled. "Damn right you will."

Billy rolled his eyes and pushed away from the stall wall. "You think you have this all figured out, don't you?"

"I think so."

"In that case, let me handcuff you next time."

"Me?"

Billy pressed his lips together to keep from laughing at the astonished look on Rourke's face. He'd bet almost anything no one had ever propositioned him in such a way. "Yes, you. You've handcuffed me often enough and had me displayed for your pleasure. Why not let me return the favor?"

"Is that something that interests you, baby?"

"It might."

"It would probably be more fun if you handcuffed my legs, too."

Now it was Billy's turn to be astonished. "You're okay with it?"

"Baby, I'm okay with anything you want to try."

"Now?"

Rourke chuckled and gestured to the horse. "Let me finish here and we can go play. Da will have my hide if this horse isn't brushed down before I put her to bed for the night."

"Can I help?"

"Hand me that brush."

Billy grabbed the brush Rourke had set down earlier and handed it over. He grinned when Rourke reached down and adjusted the thick erection bulging behind his zipper then started brushing the horse again. It was nice to know that he wasn't the only one feeling horny at the moment.

"I heard from Sheriff Riley," Rourke said absently.

"And?" Billy was surprised that his heart didn't start beating rapidly with panic at the first mention of the sheriff. He was slowly getting used to being on the right side of the law.

"Clem has been arraigned on three counts of attempted murder, one count of assault, one count of arson, and one count of kidnapping for locking you in the cellar when you tried to warn us he was going to burn down the barn."

Billy blinked. "That's a lot of charges."

"It is, but he deserves every one of them. If the judge finds him guilty, he'll be doing a lot of time. How are you going to feel about that?"

Billy shrugged.

"Billy."

Billy rolled his eyes and huffed as he pushed away from the wall and walked around to the open gate of the stall. "I don't really have any feelings about it, I guess."

"Really? None at all?"

Billy shrugged again. "Clem stopped being someone I really cared about the first time he hit me. Beyond being glad he will be locked away so that he can't hurt us anymore, I don't care. I just want him gone. I'm tired of having to watch over my shoulder all of the time."

Rourke's hand stroked the side of Billy's face. "It's hard having to live in hell, isn't it?"

Billy nodded and leaned into Rourke's hand. "It's not easy, but I'd do it again if it meant keeping you safe."

"Baby."

"Yeah, give it up, Rourke." Billy laughed. He stepped through the entrance to the stall and pushed himself into Rourke's arms. "It's not going to end anytime soon, so you'd better get used to it. It's my job to take care of you."

"You're not my keeper, baby."

"Yes, I am."

"Baby—"

"You said we belonged together and you were keeping me. That means I get to keep you, too. And that makes me your keeper."

Rourke gave Billy a quick kiss then leaned back, grinning. "You know I love you, right?"

Billy smiled. "And that makes every second I lived in hell worth it."

THE END

WWW.STORMYGLENN.COM

ABOUT THE AUTHOR

Stormy believes the only thing sexier than a man in cowboy boots is two or three men in cowboy boots. She also believes in love at first sight, soul Mates, true love, and happy endings.

Stormy lives in the great Northwest region of the USA, with her gorgeous husband and soul Mate, six very active teenagers, two boxer/collie puppies, one old biddy cat, and one fish.

You can usually find her cuddled in bed with a book in her hand and a puppy in her lap, or on her laptop, creating the next sexy man for one of her stories. Stormy welcomes comments from readers. You can find her website at www.stormyglenn.com

Also by Stormy Glenn

Blaecleah Brothers1: *Cowboys Easy*
True Blood Mate 1: *Heart Song*
True Blood Mate 2: *Alpha Born*
Wolf Creek Pack 1: *Full Moon Mating*
Wolf Creek Pack 2: *Just a Taste Of Me*
Wolf Creek Pack 3: *Tasty Treats: Volume 3, Man to Man*
Wolf Creek Pack 4: *Blood Prince*
Wolf Creek Pack 5: *Love, Always, Promise*
Wolf Creek Pack 6: *Who's Afraid of the Big Bad Wolf?*
Wolf Creek Pack 7: *Pretty Baby*
Katzman 1: *The Katzman's Mate*
Katzman 2: *Dream Mate*
Katzman 3: *Pride Mate*
Tri-Omega Mates 1: *Secret Desires*
Tri-Omega Mates 2: *Forbidden Desires*
Tri-Omega Mates 3: *Hidden Desires*
Tri-Omega Mates 4: *Stolen Desires*
Tri-Omega Mates 5: *Unspoken Desires*
Lovers of Alpha Squad 1: *Mari's Men*
Lovers of Alpha Squad 2: *The Doctor's Patience*
Lovers of Alpha Squad 3: *Julia's Knight*
Lovers of Alpha Squad 4: *Three of a Kind*
Love's Legacy 1: *Cowboy Legacy*
Love's Legacy 2: *Cowboy Dreams*
Sweet Treats
Mr. Wonderful
My Lupine Lover
The Master's Pet
Wolf Queen
His Gentle Touch
Fire Demon
Mating Heat

Also by Stormy Glenn and Joyee Flynn

Delta Wolf 1: *Chameleon Wolf*
Delta Wolf 2: *Mating Games*
Delta Wolf 3: *Blood Lust*

Available at
BOOKSTRAND.COM

Siren Publishing, Inc.
www.SirenPublishing.com

Breinigsville, PA USA
23 March 2011
258308BV00003B/71/P